My Forbidden Ghost

BAD BOY PARANORMAL ROMANCE

GHOST HEALER SERIES
BOOK ONE

ISABEAU DURANT

Contents

A Gift For Our Readers

Please follow the link for a gift of our gratitude!

> > > Click here to claim your free gift < < <

Get notified of upcoming titles by the author and publisher!

Chapter One

JMC Ranch
Coloma, California
Toes curled in anticipation, body taut with desire, I could feel him near me, and the vial of Spectressence glittered as my fingers trembled. "Oh god, don't drop it, Fiona," I whispered, willing it not to change before my eyes. This was it! It was ready. I was ready. Then I nearly dropped it. *Knock! Knock!*

"Fiona! Are you in there?" It was a Mac, my landlady. Still feeling the effects of breathing in the vapors of it, I worked to find my voice. Make it not so breathy. It had been almost five years since I last felt someone not just near me, but in me, a part of me. I'd thought he was the one. But I'd been wrong, and the moment was gone. Again.

"Come in!" I called, putting the vial gently into its wire frame holder, and took another breath as Mac appeared before me. Maisy Catherine "Mac" Wright was the co-owner of JMC Ranch here in Coloma. She owned it with her brother, Jack. Or had owned it. Past tense. Until a few months ago, when his sudden death rocked the town of Coloma and nearly sent her

1

out of business. So, she got creative, and added the title of businesswoman to rancher.

She owned JMC Ranch, one of the most well-known ranches in the area, and now infamous because her brother's sudden death had been newsworthy. It had reached the *Sacramento Bee,* where I'd briefly interned in college. Coinciding with using my biochemical degree in the agricultural industry piqued my interest. Got to admit, though, the small ad from Mac Wright about a bungalow to rent at the ranch, clinched the deal.

Coloma was a town where I could get a fresh start. It was beautiful, and had a built-in clientele for my new business, *Ghosts Gone, Home Healer.* Don't laugh. It's a working title. After all, the term clientele may have stretched the truth a bit. Mac was my first and only client. But if I could heal her haunted house, then I would be golden, a built-in referral system from the outset.

"Oh my god, what smells so good?" She eyed the array of equipment before me and shivered. "He's here, isn't he?" she asked, her blue eyes flashing.

"I think so," I said, glancing down at the vial. "I... felt him," I offered as an explanation. Felt, was putting it lightly, but the goal was to speak to him. If I could speak to ghosts, I could help them move on. Cross over into the light. Result? No unsettled ghost to haunt the living and wreak havoc on lives and businesses, which is what Jack, her brother, seemed to be doing. For someone who Mac said had always tried to help her, he had a funny way of going about it. I'd have to ask him about that. If this really, truly worked as I thought it might. So far, I'd only felt him, and that has always been my gift. The goal of Spectressence was to enhance this gift and make it more, well, practical.

Felt him. That was putting it mildly. Since I'd seen his picture in the paper, I'd had a visceral reaction to him as if he'd been standing next to me, drawing his fingers up and down my side, and the arousal that came with it. And since I'd been on the ranch, nights had become rather intense. Just thinking about it made me flush with desire, and I had to stamp it out if I wanted to keep my cool with my landlady, client, and friend.

"Oh." She took a half step back. Then, shoulders back, she stood up straighter, and bellied up to the bar, as they say. Her eyes softened. "How's it going?"

I motioned toward the dining table. "Let's sit over there and talk. Wine?" She nodded. I pulled two glasses, opened a bottle of Chardonnay, and set both on the table. Mac visibly relaxed as she realized I had been cooking food, too. Just a few tapas to nibble on while I worked and, in this case, played hostess. I poured the wine while she tasted one of my salmon croquettes.

"Honestly, I'm not sure. I had an intense connection recently, but I have only just finished putting the finishing touches on Spectressence. It's over there. Corked and safely ensconced, but there's something... I don't know. Off. Maybe it's me." I spoke between sips of wine and watched Mac's expression. It didn't change, and a realization struck. "How close were you and Jack?"

Mac took a sip of wine, closed her eyes, and smiled. "We might have been twins. That's how close we were, and I assume is why—"

"You can sense him," I finished. "Sorry." I looked down, took a croquette myself, and smiled over my mouthful. Sometimes, food is the best way to slow down the impulse to speak before listening. It's a terrible habit and unbroken; it caused me troubles, even as an adult. Especially as an adult. Food offers balance. It has its own chemistry, which is probably why I enjoy it as a hobby.

"It's not that, really. I think it's more he's working hard to ensure I know he's still around. I mean, I know you can...

feel... him. But when he makes things happen like lights flickering, doors opening and closing at all hours, it scares off customers, friends, family... me. I wish he'd consider the idea that you can't live off an income from ranching alone today. It's why I wanted to set up this B&B as part of our offerings. You're my first, and at the moment, only guest. You saw what happened the first week you stayed here. Oh, the drama! People running for the hills with Jack's antics. Don't get me wrong, I'm not afraid of him, but for someone who swore they'd help me with the ranch--." Mac stopped and looked over my shoulder as if she could see him, adding, "You're sucking at it, big brother." Then, "Hey, are you ok?" She was staring at me, eyes wide.

My eyes narrowed, and I shook my head instinctively. Following her gaze, I turned to see myself in the living room mirror and understood why she was worried. "Ohhh." The sound escaped before I could stop it. Wine glass forgotten, one hand gripped the table, knuckles turning white, and one hand, elbow up gripped the frame of the chair behind me. Somehow, a button had come loose, and my blouse opened further, teasing the eye. I swung back into position. "Fine. I'm fine." I smiled brightly and feigned nonchalance as I did up the button. Mac's eyes narrowed; one eye almost closed as she studied me.

"Talk to me, Fiona. I may not entirely understand what you do. But I know Jack, and you are his type..." she trailed off, a smile tugging at the corners of her mouth. Taking a sip of wine, she added, "The way I see it, there's more going on here than meets the eye. I may own a ranch, but I've been outside these fences, you know."

"I know that." Looking at my hands clasped tightly in my lap, I readjusted and laid arms and elbows on the small dark oak table in my little bungalow, a few steps from the farmhouse and lesser still from the stables. Frowning, it was my turn to study Mac. How much information could I tell her? Should I tell her? She's a client and a friend. Client first, I thought, and revised what I'd been about to say.

"Starting a business like mine isn't exactly something you can take to the bank and ask for a loan. It requires a certain way of thinking, of looking at things, and whatever sense you might use to interact with ghosts, the point is that ghosts leave imprints of themselves–their energy rather, that leaves an imprint–and I think that's what Jack's doing without realizing it."

"In the article I read, his death was sudden. An accidental horse kicks him in the chest leading to cardiac arrest. The paper didn't dive deeply into the cause, but seemed to focus on who, rather than what. The who, of course, being Jack Wright, gentleman rancher and rising star chemical engineer, when he took a cue from you and went back to school."

"You hired me to heal your house, and that means to get rid of entities causing the issue. In this case, Jack. But because he was born and raised here, his energy is everywhere he ever was when he was alive. So, it can be overwhelming to manage all the feelings rushing at me. This ranch has been in your family for generations, and sometimes I'm not sure if who I'm feeling is Jack. You could have other ghosts, but he's just the most prevalent. Maybe because he died young. I'm not sure."

What should I say next? I wondered. To move forward with this conversation would be more akin to talking with a friend, not a client. Talk about between two worlds. I couldn't even separate business from friendship.

I pointed to the single vial sitting in its wire case as if it were ready for a rose bud, or a water sample waiting to be tested, and smiled. "Regardless of what I think, or you think right now, we'll be able to test it."

"Spectressence?" Mac mulled over the name. "It sounds like the name of a perfume." She laughed and popped the last of the salmon croquettes in her mouth, washing it down with the last swig of wine in her glass.

"You're right. The chemical compounds that create perfume are all in there, with a few special secrets of my own for good measure. If you really want to break it down. It is 'essence of spectre' because when it works—" Mac raised her eyebrows in question.

"When. Not if?"

"Never if. Always when." I quirked my mouth and unfurled from the kitchen chair to stand by my creation. "*When* it works, I should be able to spritz it not only on myself to ensure what I'm feeling is a ghost and not just too many nights alone, but also on the ghost, allowing me to 'see' him or her. In this case, him. Jack."

The phone rang, and I glanced at the ID. Ian. I frowned and hit decline. He could wait. This couldn't.

I continued. "Once I can see and interact with the ghosts, I do what I can to encourage them to move on to the next plane, or go into the light, or whatever happens on the other side."

"You mean, you don't know?"

"How would I know?" I answered instinctively, but it didn't stop the vision. Inside the ambulance. Death was in that vehicle. And ghosts.

I was only fourteen when my first boyfriend was struck by a drunk driver. He was my best friend, too. I'd known Johnny for ten years before we had our first kiss. We'd been walking back from the park, and the car had come out of nowhere. He was just a few steps ahead of me and absorbed the initial impact of it. The people who had seen it happen called 9-1-1. Johnny came to, and I tried to tell the medics he was alive. But their words didn't match mine. It finally registered when we got to the hospital. "DOA," they said as they wheeled him out first, then me.

Mac surprised me with a quick hug as she excused herself. "Lost you there for a little while, and I know that look. Bittersweet memories, yes?" I nodded without speaking, and Mac continued. "I've taken up enough of your time already. Thanks for the wine, and the divine grub." She paused, a saucy smile on her face, "You know, if the ghost healing business doesn't work out, maybe you should open a restaurant. You've got the chops." Uh-oh, that twinkle in her eyes was back. Mac had had a reason to come, and it was more than the smell of my salmon croquettes. "I almost forgot the reason for my visit!" she slapped at her forehead with her palm. "Remember that office space in town you were asking about? I found the guy's card. The one who's leasing the space." She reached into her jeans pocket and pulled a dog-eared business card. "His name's Miller. Andrew Miller." I reached for the card, and Mac continued. "The Millers, well, just Andrew really, are part of a business cooperative helping to keep the community alive. This is such a small town, we're more like a family here."

I smiled, thinking how wonderful it was this little town endeavored to keep itself alive. It was a quiet town, but it wouldn't be a ghost town. I almost laughed. Ok, it was. But not in the way you think. Mac gave me a strange look, and I startled, remembering she'd complimented my cooking, suggesting I go into the restaurant business. *Right!* "Don't think I haven't thought about it," I said. "And thanks!" I added, taking the card. "I was glad for the company."

Mac was almost out the door when I felt his presence again. A warmth that spread from shoulders down my arms to envelop me in a hug from behind like wrapping a warm blanket around you. The warmth stopped at my stomach as if someone were laying a hand there warm and strong. "Mac!" I called. She turned.

"What's up?"

"I wanted to say thanks again for letting me rent this

darling bungalow. My next report will be more conclusive."
Mac turned back around, heading away, a backward wave, and
a dry, throaty laugh usually reserved for women much older
and bigger than Ms. Maisy Catherine Wright. No wonder she
asked to be called Mac. Her full name was a mouthful.

Closing the door, I walked back into the kitchen to pour
another glass of wine and took it into the living room. Something about the whole affair was bugging me. I liked Mac and
wondered if all my clients would be this curious and open. If
you have more clients, said my pessimistic side.

When, not if, I reminded myself and took a sip.

The mirror I'd seen myself in that showed me what Mac
saw was a huge, ox-yoke framed mirror that seemed more
Texas than California. From this angle, it showed me my vial
of Spectressence set at the front of the long bar that separated
the kitchen from the living room. Offering a prayer to the
universe for success, I studied the mirror image of everything
else I saw and formed new theories as I let my mind half
wander, half focus on what was around me.

Something caught the corner of my eye as I sipped at the
wine. It was a form, caught in the fading sunbeams through
the window reflected in the mirror. Nature's Spectressence,
and the inspiration behind my formula. "Is that really you,
Jack?" I asked the form in the mirror. "Or is it another spectre,
ghost, whatever, who's trying to get my attention?" I thought
I heard a laugh that could have been the male version of Mac's,
but it was gone almost as soon as I'd registered it.

Then, the record player in the corner began crackling, and
the sounds of "Pancho and Lefty" on vinyl streamed through
the speakers. I laughed, got up, and put the needle back in its
pocket. "Sorry, I need to concentrate. You can play later."

The last of the sun dipped down below the horizon as I sat
back down on the sofa. Was I crazy? That had been the
consensus in the university circles, one name in particular

notwithstanding. Maybe I was. But you don't make history by sitting on your tush, my great aunt had said, and she would know. She may not be in the history books, but her achievements are. She was an activist, an engineer, and writer, holding patents on things as basic as the rollers to feed paper through more easily on a typewriter.

I am crazy. I've put every cent I have into starting a business to heal haunted houses from their unwelcome guests. Ghosts. But the perks are well worth it, especially when the ghost in question is Jack Wright. Had it been his picture that drew me to read the article? He was handsome. That was undeniable. Had it been he happened to be a ghost that moved me to a small town in northern California? Whenever he was near, did I feel lit up like a Christmas tree?

Yes, to all the above. Just one problem. He was a ghost, and I had a shadow.

Chapter Two

A s if on cue, the phone rang. "Yes?" I answered, clicking the green button without looking at the ID, my eyes firmly fixed on the expanse of night sky from my window.

"Fiona?"

"Ian." My breath sharpened, and I felt a familiar tension. "I'm not coming back, Ian. I'm building a life here."

"Building? No. Running? Yes. Regardless, that's not why I called." He took a breath, and I rushed in, "Why did you call me, then?"

"Hey, you invited me. I'm calling to let you know I'll be there tomorrow afternoon. Late."

"Tomorrow? Where are you now?" I worried my lip and began tapping my fingers nervously on my leg. There was too much going on here. I was too close to proving my theory. Did I really need Ian here? Plus, I was staying with my client, well, on her property anyway. I sighed and straightened my shoulders. I could handle Dr. Ian Quigley *and* Jack Wright. At the same time. I am woman... hear me roar. Ha!

"Sacramento," Ian choked back a laugh. "Where else would I be?"

"Sacramento," I repeated dumbly. Fingers snapped in my ear, and I bristled, but kept my mouth shut. Maybe I should have said something and kept this conversation short. But it didn't work that way with Ian. His voice begged to be listened to, which is probably why most of the students in his classes were women. Who knew Dr. Ian Quigley would drive women into the fields of science and agriculture. For half a second, I wondered if Mac had taken any of his classes when she'd gone back to school last year. "Better late than never," she'd said at my surprise.

"Fiona, focus. Or are you distracted by one of your ghosts?"

"They're not MY ghosts. I'm haunted enough, but they are somebody's ghost, and here, it's just one."

"Have you met him? Her? It? What do you call them if you can't see them?"

"Well, the client tells me, who—"

The line crackled, and Ian pealed with laughter. "Who! Who! Woo! Woo!"

"Stop it! You're acting like a child."

"I-I'm-I'm acting like a—" he sputtered between laughs. "Fine. Think what you want. But we need to talk."

"We already talked, and you made it quite clear what you think of my life's work."

"Fiona," his voice softened, "this isn't someone's life work. This is a child's flight of fancy with grown up toys. Me. I'm real. It's just utterly improbable that living beings can interact with ghosts at any level: visceral, emotional, physical, or otherwise. I'm a scientist. I deal in facts. You did, too. Once."

Shutting my eyes, I counted to ten. I could hear him breathing, waiting for me to break the silence. Well, he could wait ten seconds.

"Listen, I don't want to fight. We've done enough of that.

Don't you think?" I nodded in answer, not caring he couldn't see me.

"No. I mean, yes. Yes. We've done enough fighting." For one day, anyway. My thoughts finishing what I couldn't say. How did it come to this? We'd been friends, colleagues. Lovers. And that's where it went to pot. Had we gotten too close? Is that even possible?

"What are you afraid of, Fiona?" Ian asked. He didn't sound patronizing, only concerned. Well, that was a switch.

"I'm not afraid of anything. I just needed a fresh start. After...." I let the words hang in the air. He'd finish my thought, he always did.

"After the fire." He added in a soft voice.

"Yes," I said, and images of the fire, the press, and the trauma of becoming a laughingstock in the one place I'd once felt safe came flooding back.

"That was a terrible accident..." He paused, unsure. Very un-Ian. Was he protecting my feelings or his?

"That could have been prevented if I hadn't rushed the experiment for Spectressence, and blown up the lab. Yes, I know. I was there, thanks." I paused for the space of a heartbeat and continued. "And before you start, I realize not only did I cause a catastrophic blow to the lab, but to my career as well. I heard enough from my parents. I don't need to hear it from you, too." I'd been pacing as I spoke, and looked down to see a well-worn path in the old wooden flooring of the bungalow. Seems I wasn't the only one who paced when upset.

"I'm not judging, I never did." Ian's voice was somber, not placating or pleading. "You know, I'm still trying to get to know you. You're not the open book you think you are. In fact, if you were a library book, I'd find you locked away behind glass in the restricted section. You're not fragile, but you're not open either. Is that why you'd rather play with—

sorry—interact with ghosts? Once they're gone, they're out of your hair. Help me out. I'm trying to understand."

Listening to Ian, I knew he was right, but I wasn't about to tell him. Talk about feeding the beast. Somehow, in my pacing, I'd settled into a little window seat in the hallway between the living room and the bedroom. It had been a long day, and I needed sleep. Did I really need Ian Quigley here tomorrow to complicate things? I had a job to do, regardless of his thoughts on the matter.

"Do you remember the first time we met?" He asked, pretending I hadn't been silent for too long. Before I could answer, he finished. "You were hiding yourself behind goggles, a lab coat, sensible shoes, and your hair pulled back into one of those messy bun things."

"Wow, I must have looked a sight!" I laughed remembering that day. "I wasn't the only one hiding in a lab coat and goggles, you know."

"Touché. Anyway, you took one look at my nametag and dubbed me 'Einstein.'"

"I remember. It was your initials—IQ. Ian Quigley. I like to think I was trying to say 'hi' but was too distracted--."

"Oh, I like where this is going. But I digress. What I've been trying to say is that even with your lab coat on and hair up, I thought you were the most beautiful woman I'd ever seen. I didn't even realize how red your hair was until I saw it down two nights later. Somehow, you made a lab coat sexy, and then I was the one who couldn't concentrate."

I knew where this was going. Classic Quigley. Frustrate, then turn on the charm, and of course, change the subject.

"I'm still mad at you."

"Then why did you invite me?"

"I don't know."

"Yes, you do. I am no ghost. I am a human man with human wants and desires." Ian's voice was thick with emotion, and I could almost feel the heat of his body through the phone.

"And to save the damsel in distress. Save your superhero for someone else." The words were out before I realized, and I'd meant them to sting. But in classic Quigley fashion, he took it as a challenge. Shocker!

"You think Einstein is a superhero?" Ian asked, chuckling. "Only you, would think that."

"You know what I mean, Ian," I said through clenched teeth. Oh, that man could make my blood boil, and knew what buttons to push. He knew nearly all of me. But it was the most important part he couldn't grasp.

"Maybe tomorrow's too soon," he said, thoughtfully. "But I know you want me there. We work well together, though we don't always agree."

"This is different. But, yes, I need—want—you here." I need you to see it work. That's why I wanted him there. The tension in the bungalow was palpable, and I was the only one there. Or was I? No, Jack wasn't here with me. I hadn't felt his presence since early this evening. Not tonight. Tilting my head, I studied a picture of the Wright family taken years before. It was the entire clan. Jack and Mac stood in front, while their parents, JD and Eleanor, stood behind them, hands resting protectively on their children's shoulders.

"Ian, I don't care when you come. But it's been a long day, and I need to get some sleep."

"Your camera's on." *Shit!* I knew where this was going. All you have to do is hang up, Fiona, and then he goes away. Poof! Well, until tomorrow anyway. I knew that voice, deep and throaty. There was a hint of something else behind it tonight, though I couldn't put my finger on it. Jealousy? Maybe. But that wasn't Ian's style.

"How? Oh, I must have hit the button when I was looking at the picture." I knew I was rambling. Ian once had that kind of hold over me. Looks like he still does, added a nagging voice. The same voice that had told me to get out of dodge after the fire.

"Your beautiful red hair. Why are you hiding it in a ponytail? You're going to bed, right? Let me see it down." What could it hurt?

"Okay. I've got to put the phone down first. This operation requires two hands." I propped the phone up on the vanity. Mac had done a grand job of making the old bunkhouse into a homey bungalow. She'd thought of every detail.

"Mmm… fine. That's fine." Ian's face appeared on the screen. His blonde hair and mismatched eyes, one blue, one brown, watched in appraisal. "So, what are you wearing to bed?" He could be direct, that's for sure.

"None of your business," I teased. "But since you asked, let me slip into…"

"Something more comfortable?" He asked eagerly.

"My closet." I looked at him pointedly, eyebrows raised, and pointed at the closet. "I'm going to change… In there." The dramatic breath he released was so comical I would have laughed, if I hadn't known it was strictly for show. "You'll just have to use your imagination."

"I am a scientist. We don't have imaginations." He paused, a twinkle in his eye. "Well, you do." I raised an eyebrow at him, and he added, "Have an imagination. Who else would think they could--." I cut him off.

"Don't start. As for scientific imaginations or lack thereof, I'm calling bull. Wasn't it Einstein who said, 'creativity is intelligence having fun'? See? Imagination," I called from the closet, as I changed from jeans and a white blouse to a cream short set I'd found at a boutique in downtown Coloma the day I arrived in town. It occurred to me, fleetingly, that I had, however, yet to wear it. Stepping from the closet, I caught my reflections in the vanity mirror where I'd propped the phone, and saw what Ian saw.

In the short few months I'd been in Coloma, my legs and body were bronzing in the California sun, which set off the creamy nightwear. There was a glow in my cheeks that disproved the need for any makeup. The top was a comfortable fit, though sizes and I didn't always see eye to eye. According to my mother and Ian, I was well proportioned. If I'd had ombre hair instead of red, Ian had said once, I might have been mistaken for a forty-something Sofia Vergara.

"Wow!" Ian's voice carried across the room. "Maybe I'll come tomorrow after all."

I sat down at the vanity and began to brush my hair. "How is it you make the simple act of brushing your hair look sexy?" Ian asked, his eyes wide, and shaking his head in bewilderment.

"Stop it. I said I was getting ready for bed." I held up my brush. "This is just one step in the routine. You may not like some of the other steps as much."

"I'll be fine. Let me watch you." He tilted his head far to the side in an exaggerated manner which made me laugh. "Perfect," he breathed. "I wanted to hear you laugh. It's been too long, Fiona Perry."

"Too long," I repeated, turning to look him in the eyes. Miles separated us, but our connection ran deep. Many of our memories were good. "Ian," I said, softly. "You can come tomorrow if you want."

"Tomorrow," he said. He held my gaze, and a lifetime passed between us. "I don't know if I can... wait... until tomorrow, Fiona. I still care for you, want you. I've missed you."

Swallowing, my tongue and throat felt tight. All I could say was, "Yes, Ian. To all of it." I felt my body flush and asked, "Is it getting hot in here or am I just hot flashing?"

"No. It's hot over here, too," Ian said, removing his shirt.

"Your turn," he said, a curt nod toward me. "I'm having trouble controlling…"

"Not tonight, Ian. Tomorrow. In person." I reached to hit the red button to hang up. "Wait!" he shouted. "Let me look at you a little longer. Please." The last word was an effort. Ian didn't say please lightly.

"I'm going to *sleep,* Einstein." In a move designed to make him sweat, I began to unbutton my top, just a few buttons, and let my hair fall suggestively. "You can wait until tomorrow." Smiling, I ended the call. But the lingering arousal from our brief chat wouldn't end so quickly. Tomorrow couldn't get here soon enough.

Chapter Three

I hadn't bothered to close the curtains, and the early dawn streamed into my window. The blush of the sun peeking over the horizon beckoned me, and I pressed my face to the glass. A walk would be good. I could clear my head. Had it been the wine talking last night when I encouraged Ian to come for a visit? "Hmm, I wonder what he wants," I mused as I walked back into the closet to get ready for the day. A few minutes later, checking myself in the mirror, I admired the long, deep-blue, formfitting maxi dress. "Ugh, what I am I doing?" You're getting ready for Ian, a little voice nagged. Or maybe someone, or something else. Retracing my steps, I traded the formfitting dress for a robin's egg blue sundress and sneakers. Better!

I grabbed a light jacket and was out the door, following the sign toward the trail Mac had pointed out upon my arrival. "It's a bridle trail," she'd explained. "But if you're up early enough, you shouldn't run into anyone."

Inhaling the fresh air, I felt a cool breeze lift the hem of my dress as I walked, heading toward the river's edge. As I walked, I thought about Jack, and wondered what was making him stay at the ranch. Why was he making such a big stink? He had to know it was bad for business, and it wasn't helping Mac get past his death. He needed to move on.

She knew it was him, Mac had said when she'd hired me. Jack seemed to move only certain items, or Mac would hear a special knock they'd made up as children. Then there were the horses. It was as if they could still see him. "It's freaking me out, Ms. Perry," Mac had said. "And I don't scare so easily."

"Call me Fiona," I'd said, feeling an instant connection to this woman I barely knew, and a now dead man I didn't know at all.

I'd been so deep in thought; I didn't realize I'd turned around and skipped up the steps to Mac's front porch. She was a rancher, she'd be awake. The bottom of the sun still touched the horizon, and I shaded my eyes to see better.

"Morning, Mac!" I said, waving. She'd been out gathering eggs by the basket, one on each arm. "C'mon, I can help you know. I grew up on a ranch. Did I tell you?" I planted my hands on my hips and tried to stifle a laugh, declaring, "I have a master's degree from Cal State."

"Morning, Fiona! Aren't you bright and cheery this morning? Who plumed your feathers?" She asked, her eyes sparkling. Pointedly ignoring my declaration. I stretched my arms out as if to embrace the sky, smiling ear to ear. Before I could answer, she indicated the baskets of eggs, raising each arm. "Breakfast?"

"Sure, I'll cook." I took one basket from her and headed for the door.

"I was hoping you'd say that! I've never eaten so well having you around. Maybe you were a chuck wagon cook in a previous life or something." Mac teased as she skirted around me and went into the kitchen to set her own basket down.

"What are you going to do with all these eggs? Are you

expecting more company?" I asked as she reached for a couple of empty egg cartons.

"No, not till I'm sure it's clear. Afraid it's just you and me until then, Chica. But I am going into town, and will deliver a couple of dozen to the karma kitchen." She stopped loading each egg into its holder and her hazel eyes caught my blue ones. "I thought maybe while I was away you could test... what do you call it?"

"Spectressence." I confirmed.

"Right. Test your Spectressence and see what is up with my big brother. What the hell is keeping him here?" Mac frowned and stared down at a half empty carton. She quirked her mouth, "He's the only man I know who hated eggs, but loved haggis. Weird, huh?" Shaking her head, Mac continued until she had filled both cartons.

"Did he travel abroad or something?"

"No. I think he just wanted to be different. He was born into ranching, though his passion was building things, or rather engineering them." Mac shrugged. "But he could ride a horse, tame a stud, and had a way with animals no one could fathom. He wasn't quite like a horse whisperer, but he came close." She slammed a hand on the countertop. "Which is why it's so weird, he died from a horse kicking him! How does that happen?" Mac turned toward me, tears in her eyes.

"Hey," I took her hands in mine. "That's why I'm here. Why you hired me." I'd been breaking and stirring eggs, prepping them for a couple of omelets as she'd been talking. "Listen, why don't you go deliver your eggs, and let me do some work in here. Sometimes, ghosts can be more prevalent in one room versus another, but since you said you felt him here, first, I'll start in your house. If I need to, I'll take Spectressence and see what happens in the bungalow. You said it used to be the bunkhouse, right?"

"Yeah," Mac wiped her eyes. "After Jack died, I couldn't

look at the place. Considered burning it down more than once. Until I realized I was feeling sorry for myself. Our parents are gone. It was just me and Jack. Mac and Jack. How corny is that?" Mac laughed, and added, "But I couldn't destroy it. My parents would have come back to haunt to tell me how wasteful I was being. So, I kept the bones of it, and turned it into a bungalow. It was a way to make some extra money and get rid of reminders of everything... everyone I'd lost." Mac looked at her watch and hiked the tote on shoulder a little tighter.

I winced, "Eggs," I reminded her in a soft voice as if my voice would remind her of the fragility of her cargo.

"Sorry, I'll leave you to it." She adjusted her grip, skirted around the counter, and headed toward the door. Opening it, she turned to look at me, and added, "It's probably more than you needed to know about the Wright Family of JMC Ranch. But maybe it will help you finish your work here. I love my brother. But I need him to go." She raised her eyes to the right thinking, searching. "To move on, I mean. I'll be back in a few hours. I may meet up with some friends too, to give you plenty of time alone with... Jack." Her voice cracked, and she strode to her car, got in, and drove off without looking back. I closed the door behind her.

Returning to the kitchen and the nearly forgotten mixing bowl of eggs, I whisked in a splash of heavy cream, a little dill, pepper, and a dash of salt. A pat of butter in the pan on medium heat, and pour the concoction into the pan. As the liquid began to set, I tested to see when it might be ready to be flipped. Now. The eggs would set in a few more seconds, then I flipped the omelet, and slid it onto a plate. I put one plate in the fridge with a note. "I'd promised breakfast. Put it back in the pan to reheat. Do not microwave!" I put mine on a plate and set it on the counter, intending to carry it across to the bungalow. I wasn't sure if I'd feel Jack here, or if his presence was more prevalent in what had once been the bunkhouse. We'd just have to see.

"Looks like it's just you and me, Jack," I said, wondering if he'd appear if I spoke out loud. There didn't seem to be any rhyme or reason to his appearances, so I had no real baseline to begin. Well, unless I counted the brief encounter in the bungalow last night. He'd appeared then. I reached into the front pocket of the skirt of my sundress and retrieved the vial of Spectressence. Time to get this party started.

Mac had never mentioned where she'd felt his presence specifically, so I wandered from room to room taking in everything around me. In the bathroom, I found a small vial with a spritzer cap and poured Spectressence into it, praying the plastic didn't somehow dilute anything. Until now, I'd put it in a glass vial, and had a sudden vision of glass crashing, splintering, and spilling across Mac's flooring. I clutched the new vial tighter after re-corking and slipped my vial back into my skirt pocket. Holding the Spectressence, trigger finger at the ready, I continued my tour of the ranch house.

It was long and narrow, with rooms on each side down a long hallway interspersed with a bathroom or two; the kitchen, living and dining room combo, one vast space on one end, and a kind of solarium at the other end. Someone had liked their plants, and all the space outside wasn't enough.

Mac had piled a stack of books high against a chaise longue for reading, and an open magazine, bookmarked by being turned upside down to keep it open, decorated the only seat in the room. Native plants created an indoor garden, and spices planted into one of those wall-hanging herb planters decorated two walls. The other two walls were floor to ceiling windows. It was an oasis.

It was in this room I felt him. "Jack?" I called. "Was this your place? The solarium?" No answer. But the fluttering of another magazine's pages called my attention to it. *Horse &*

Rider. "I know you're here, Jack. You're trying to make contact, aren't you?" My voice wavered slightly. Mostly, ghosts didn't frighten me, but this ghost made my body tingle. He was near. I could feel him.

I sprayed the Spectressence somewhere between the chaise and one of the glass walls. Backlit by the sun, I could *see* him. Well, almost. He was a shadow in reverse, the negative image in a film roll, but more light than dark. He'd been leaning against the glass, one leg propped up behind him, hat in his hand. Waiting.

"Ma'am" His voice was faint as if speaking from the opposite end of a tunnel. "You can see me!" Then, "You are a vision." He tilted his head. "Are you one of Mac's friends? I would have remembered you." His voice strengthened as he came nearer.

My breath stopped, a quick gasp, and he was standing before me. Shimmering. "Fiona," I gasped as he took my wrists in his hands. "Fiona Perry." I felt feather light fingertips caress my wrists, then fingers wrapped themselves around my arms and moved up to my shoulders. Like liquid mercury in a thermometer, my body heat rose.

"It is lovely to meet you, Ms. Fiona Perry." Oh god, I was losing control. Hold on, Fiona! Keep it together. This. Is. For. *Science*. His form stepped ever closer, growing stronger as I lost sense of time. Suddenly, he was around me, behind me, embracing me. Silver arms entwined with mine, stroking, caressing, cool breath on my neck. My body stretched to breaking. Ready, taut. Wanting.

Then, just as quickly as he'd appeared, he was gone.

I deflated like a balloon and crumpled into the chaise, my body pushing the upside-down magazine onto the floor. My heart raced. My breathing quick and shallow. In between breaths, I wondered what it would be like to be on the other side. Suddenly, I heard Ian, as if he'd heard my thoughts.

"You're on the side you're supposed to be. With me. I'm human. Here for you, now."

The visceral response of my body's echoes of Jack imagined a warmer grip, stronger hands, and no sudden stops. Head stretched back, I put the back of my hand against my forehead, as if in a swoon, and sat upright. Sweat dampened my hair, and my hands were shaking. Was that real? It felt like it, and would have been more intense if he hadn't suddenly pulled back. Oh god, had I thought about Ian when Jack was around? Had he sensed another? Like male dogs sniffing out a bitch in heat.

The image made me laugh, and I stood up with a last look at the glass wall from which Jack had materialized when I sprayed Spectressence. I've always felt aroused when ghosts were around, but this one was different. I just couldn't put my finger on it. This encounter was intense, and one I wanted to repeat. "Except that you have a very much alive man coming to see you today," I reminded myself, imagining Ian doing what the ghost had started.

Who was I kidding? I'd been on tenterhooks since the video call with Ian last night. I was ripe for the taking, in this world and the next. Had all that really happened in just a few minutes? It had felt like hours. The wall clock kept its secrets.

A single question remained. Was he really gone? Had Jack left JMC Ranch? Only one way to find out.

Chapter Four

I groped for the vial again and sprayed it in the same direction as the first time. No ghost. Spritzing and spraying in shotgun fashion, I turned slowly, focusing on each wall. At one point, I thought I heard a chuckle, and dismissed the thought just as quickly. I had to be sure. There was more riding on this than money, though that was a sizeable chunk of my anxiety. Reputation, though. It hung by a thread. If I ever wanted to enter the doctorate program at Cal State, and beyond that, a professorship, well... life as I knew it depended on the success of Spectressence.

Sprsh! I aimed at the doorway to cover all my bases, and when nothing materialized, flush with excitement, I danced a little jig. Here it was, proof of concept! My biochemical spray that began its life in a lab fire, had come to fruition in the kitchen of my client's haunted house's adjacent bungalow. I wanted to shout it from the rooftops, then a memory of Ian's voice broke into my thoughts. An old, worn-out argument resurfaced, and had been the catalyst that drove me from Sacramento to Coloma for a fresh start.

"Why are you so hellbent on creating something to prove

ghosts exist? What are you trying to prove, and to whom?" He'd asked in the café that day, looking at his glass of red wine and watching it swirl, rather than at me. I didn't have an answer. At least, not one he would understand.

"Because I can't believe that everyone leaves this place as soon as they die. Some stick around. Whether they have something to say, to do, to see, I don't know. But I know they're there. I can…" Eyes cast down, I smoothed my ankle length green dress, feeling the straps stretch against my shoulders. I didn't know how to finish the sentence. Could I tell him I felt ghosts the way I felt him when he was near? He'd never understand. But there was a science to it. There had to be. The entire universe is numbers. Why not ghosts?

"What? Talk to them? See them? Feel them?" His words came rapid fire trying to spark an argument. It worked.

"You don't think I can do it, do you? Am I crazy? Maybe. But I've gotten so close I can taste it!" Hands clenched by my side; I headed toward the door. "If you don't have faith in me and what I can do, then you can find someone else to-to-." Struggling for the words, I shook my head fighting back angry tears. Couldn't he see I was almost in pieces? He moved in and took me in his arms.

"Fiona, relax. I am on your side. I just don't understand why you're trying so hard with this. Last week, this experiment of yours nearly killed you! You were alone in the lab. Which you know is against university protocol. And the fire, the explosion endangered others' lives. It's not like you. This isn't you. At least, not the Fiona *I* know."

I twisted from his grasp. "That's just it, Dr. Ian. You don't know me. That's the point—"

"You think a ghost could know you better?" Ian's eyebrows raised to his hairline, incredulous.

"That's not what I mean, and you know it. But I have money behind this. All the savings I have left after—." Oh god, was that why I was trying to prove ghosts existed. I'd lost him so long ago; I'd never truly made the connection.

"After what, Fiona." He bent down to look me in the eye. I tried to look away, but he cupped my face and guided me back to him. "Or is it, after who? Is that what all this is about? Did you lose someone, and you've been trying to—what---get them back from beyond the grave?" The corners of his mouth quirked in a half smile fighting to stay serious. "You know this isn't healthy, Fi. Maybe you should talk with someone."

"I am. I was," I breathed the words so softly, I wondered if he'd heard. No therapist could help, I knew. What kind of scientist believes in ghosts?

* * *

"Fiona?" A woman's voice broke into my reverie. It was Mac returning from her errands. "Hey, are you okay? Can I get you something?" Her creased brow made me wonder what I must have looked like when she walked in, but before I could answer, she changed tack. Mac sniffed. "Oh my god, I forgot. You made breakfast, didn't you? And I just ran off..." She dropped her head. "I'm awful. I didn't think. We just started talking about Jack and I had to get out of the house. Get away."

I smiled wanly, then I remembered where I was, and what had happened. "Mac!" The success of Spectressence came flooding back to me and I beamed at her, slapping my thigh. "I made breakfast. Your plate is in the fridge." I checked my watch. "You weren't gone too long; it should still be okay. I hope." Eyes dancing, I stood up, "But that's not the best news!"

"Breakfast, or I guess brunch or lunch now, isn't the best news... Wait..." Mac inhaled sharply. "Did it work? In here?

This house." She crooked a finger toward the ceiling and spun in a slow circle.

"It did!" Adopting a somber tone, though a smile played at my lips, I took Mac's hands in mine, and said, "I assure you that as of less than an hour ago, your haunted home has healed of its ghosts."

"You are amazing!" Grasping me in a bear hug, she repeated thank you like a mantra.

* * *

Back at the bungalow, I celebrated with a glass of red wine at the bistro table under a shade tree. Raising my glass, I toasted the ghost of Jack Wright. The clock in the kitchen struck twelve and I let my mind wander.

Two of the most sensual encounters I'd had in a while, had been with a ghost. Intense, but not physical. Still, there was a connection. Would it have been there still if he'd been alive? Maybe. But who really knew what might have been? A random kick from a horse had killed him almost instantly. Now, he was gone again. This time for good, according to the results of Spectressence. Yet, here I was, having just completed a job for my first client, and I had regrets. Closing my eyes, I let the day's rays wash over me, and felt its kiss. Its intimate, familiar touch. Hiking my dress up my thighs as far as I dared, the sun followed the same path on my legs as the ghost of Jack had done on my arms in the solarium.

"Ian is real," I said into the glass as I set it down on the table, and let it languish between my fingers, spinning it on its stem between them. "And yet I can't shake these feelings for someone I barely know. Someone who is now gone. He no longer exists, thanks to my experiment." A warm breeze made ripples in the wine and the hairs on the back of my neck tingled. I stopped twirling and lifted the glass to my lips, drained it; a new question on my mind.

Who was I without Spectressence? Who was I, now that it worked, and I could move forward with my ghost healing business which I still had yet to name. When it wasn't my singular focus because I'd now proven it worked, and I was right all along.

* * *

"Fiona Perry," I rolled the name on my tongue and tasted the silkiness of her skin. I wondered if her red hair flagged her as a spitfire, and almost wished against this. It was her vulnerability and openness that had me wanting more of her. I knew she wanted me too. I'd felt it. Her. The electricity between us could cause some dangerous sparks. She thought she'd gotten rid of me. Not on your life. I was staying put.

Maybe I'd leave Mac alone. But only if she'd leave Fiona to me. Death suddenly had an upside.

Chapter Five

Ian pulled up just as I'd changed back into my dark blue maxi dress. Seems I'd been expecting his arrival more than I cared to admit today. Or maybe it was just the echoes of being so close to Jack. Yes, I realize he's a ghost. But that hadn't stopped either of us, had it?

"Hello!" I waved as Ian put his yellow Lotus Elise into park next to my green VW bug. I know they say, 'clothes make the man', but in Ian's case, it's more like the car makes the man, or at least represents the man, body and soul. While I'd been contemplating his choice of car, Ian had gotten out, grabbed his suitcase, and was catching me up in a bear hug, his lips ready for a welcoming kiss. A shadow passed over his face as I gave him a peck on the cheek. I wasn't ready for the full commitment of the kiss he wanted. Not yet.

I couldn't get those echoes of my time with Jack in the solarium out of my head. No one can be in two places at once, least of all me. But I had company now, so it was time to dust off my hostess skills and welcome him here. If he wanted to be with me, he'd have to get used to my adoptive town, and this bungalow.

"Fiona?" I looked at him. "Did you hear anything I said?" My eyes widened, and I realized I'd been so caught up in trying to keep my thoughts and feelings separate, I hadn't heard a thing.

"Sorry. I've got a lot on my mind right now. What's up?"

"I was just saying it was a beautiful drive up, and we should check out some of the other little towns in the area too. Or maybe plan a camping trip along the river?" Ian hugged me again, and I kissed him without answering.

"Let's get you in the bungalow and set up. Mac's set me up with a great selection of wine from Napa, and the chef," I mimed putting on a chef's hat, "is in. What would you like for dinner? You must be hungry."

"I could eat. Whatever you make is worth it, so... surprise me." Good, I could focus on the food and use that time to sort myself out before things get too crazy.

Dinner went well. Better than expected, and in a surprise twist, Ian said nothing disparaging about my work, the accident, or call me cuckoo for believing I could talk to ghosts. Little did he know. Ha!

"Ian, I've got some errands to do around the ranch. Will you be okay for a couple of hours?" I asked as we finished eating.

"I'm a big boy, Fi. I'll be fine."

As part of my work-stay arrangement, what I said was true, but I was worried about the hauntings, and couldn't let him know. "I know. But, if anything happens, Mac is straight down that path." I pointed at the ranch house across the gravel path. He could call out if he needed to. Despite that, there was something about Jack's disappearance that didn't sit right. I could still *feel* him, even if I couldn't see him.

"You know," Ian said. "If you're that worried about me, I could just go with you." He paused, "unless there's another reason you don't want me tagging along."

It wasn't a bad idea, but I didn't want him following me checking and double-checking Mac's ghost was gone. I'd be all over the ranch, in and out of her house, and the outbuildings. I didn't need a shadow.

"No, Ian. It's better if you stay here." I glanced out the window. "There's still plenty of daylight left this evening, if you want to take a walk down to the river. I can meet you there when I'm finished."

He pressed his lips together. "Okay."

I grabbed a denim jacket from the coat rack and threw it around my shoulders. "I'll be back in a couple of hours. Help yourself to whatever's here," I said over my shoulder as I left.

But everywhere I went, Ian appeared. Trees along the path. Behind me as I entered the rooms in Mac's house. He even followed me into the stables. "Aren't you afraid of horses?" I asked when he appeared. Ian shrugged but said nothing. He must have left seconds after me, but without my hearing him. Who knew he could be so stealthy?

Finally, I'd had enough. "Ian," I said when he came in step with me on the path toward the river. "I have *work* to do. Part of my rent here is helping Mac around the ranch. She's working on a new feed for the horses and I'm advising her from a biochemist standpoint. So, if you're following me hoping to catch me talking to a ghost, you're out of luck." I held out my hands palm up. "Sorry."

What I didn't tell him was about my encounter with Jack, that I could talk to ghosts, and could prove it. I also didn't tell him what Jack, and I did while we were talking. Those feelings were all over the place. I mean, c'mon, who falls for a ghost? Had I fallen for him? What exactly did I feel when I wasn't feeling everything all at once? I had myself to sort out before I could sort out anything with Ian.

I turned on my heel and headed back to the bungalow. "I need some wine. You?"

"Yeah." Ian reached for my shoulder, and I stopped. "Hey, are you okay?"

"You are the second person to ask me that today. Why does everyone think there's something wrong with me?" Fluster and worry must have flashed across my face. Mac had asked, too, and right after I'd been with Jack. Did I have a certain look when meeting ghosts? I'd have to bring a mirror or something next time. Next time. Would there be a next time? I'd gotten rid of him, hadn't I?

I let out a breath, and my shoulders relaxed. "Like I said, Ian. I've got a lot on my mind." I locked eyes with him, "Above and beyond my experiment. I know that's why you followed me. You wanted to see it in action."

"No, Fiona. I want to see *you* in action. I think I've made it pretty clear that I couldn't care less about ghosts. I am a scientist. I believe in what I can see, touch, and feel." His arm snaked around my waist, and he pulled me to him roughly, his lips on mine, hard.

"Mmm…" His name was on my mind, but I couldn't form it. He was everything warm and solid that Jack wasn't. My body was at attention. So was his. Without realizing it, we'd walked back to the bungalow. Ian lifted me in his arms and carried me across the threshold. "Is this bad luck if we're not married?" I whispered, giggling.

"No. It's only bad luck if I drop you." I swatted at his arm and he laughed. Suddenly, he raised his eyebrows. "In case you weren't sure, you kissed me back, you know." He waited and jerked his head toward the door. "Out there. Your kiss matched mine. So, now let's see if we can… match… other things." His voice was strained.

"Put me down, Ian. We're inside now," I whispered. When he did, I reached for him. "Come," I said leading him toward the bedroom. Once in the bedroom, he untied my dress. I reached for his shirt, untucked it from his pants, loosening his belt, unbuttoning. Together, we worked each other out of our clothes, and came together in bed.

I loosed everything I'd been holding back. Breasts, once taut against my dress, pillowed against his chest. Ian's powerful arms lifting me, our bodies one, dancing to a song only we could hear.

The music sped up, and we followed in kind. Primal release.

Chapter Six

"I'll show you the town," I said, cheerily reaching for Ian's hand. "You'll see the magic here that I see, I know you will." Though freshly showered and changed, I was still flush with excitement and wanted to find other outlets for this nervous energy. Ian and I had come together again as easily as the first time we'd made love in college. Were we college sweethearts? I guess you could say so, though our twenties were well behind us.

But my drive to prove ghosts existed. That I could feel and speak to them... well, from a purely scientific perspective, years later, that had driven one heck of a wedge between us. Until now.

"Sure," he said. "There's something I want to talk to you about, anyway." His eyes sparkled, and I squeezed his hand in agreement.

* * *

How could she just *leave* like that! Their unmade bed a reminder of her with another man, and I saw red. What had the ancient Celts called it? The red mist. But with no soul to reign in my wrath, I settled for the next best thing. A temper tantrum.

Rage knocked a hole in the bedroom wall above the headboard. Drawers flew open as frustration and anger battled, clothes and papers flying, pictures ripped from the walls, glass shattered from my cold bellowed primal scream that no one could hear.

Floorboards ripped from their tongue-and-groove planking; knives buried in the walls. Sis had done a good job with the marble countertops. Anger spent, I found myself back in the solarium. My copy of *Horse & Rider*, and inside, a hidden copy of *Popular Mechanics*, still lay in a puddle of pages where Fiona had pushed them from the chaise when she'd swooned after our sensual encounter.

* * *

"Fiona," Ian dabbed his mouth with his napkin, placed it in his lap, then lightly adjusted the restaurant's plate setting at his seat. He moved his wineglass to the right, untouched.

"What do you want, Ian? And stop stalling." Leaning forward, I placed my chin on my hands, elbows on the table. I knew it drove him crazy, but crazy was my middle name these days, so I gave a mental shrug, and leaned in further. "I don't really remember inviting you out here. You..." I searched for the right word. "Confuse me."

He laughed. "I confuse you?" he asked stressing the word you as if half wishing I could read his mind so he wouldn't have to say anything. Ian shook his head. "Humans are complex individuals, aren't we? But oddly simple at the same time. It is a conundrum from time immemorial." He took a sip of his wine. "Anyway, I'll cut to the chase."

"You always do," I murmured. He snorted.

"Listen, I've missed you. We have fun together, don't we?" Ian smiled his rakish half smile and ran a hand through his hair. "Come back to the city with me, Fi. Things will be—are —different." He looked around at the diners and out the window. "This is a beautiful town. You were right about that, and I would love to come back to visit. But you belong in the city. With me." He'd reached across the table and taken my hands in his, his thumbs rubbing my wrist, adding words he didn't realize he was saying. I missed him, sure. But I wanted to be more than a warm body in a bed. I was more than a warm body in a bed. Extricating myself from his touch, I took a sip of wine to calm my nerves. I had to tell him what had happened yesterday before he arrived.

"Ian," I said, my voice hushed. "I did it."

"You did what?"

"Spectressence *works!* I proved it yesterday at Mac's house." His brow furrowed, and I sighed. Relationships work better when both sides listen to the other. But I wasn't into changing people, I was still working on myself. "Maisy Catherine Wright. Her nickname is Mac. She owns the ranch and is renting me the bungalow. Remember now?" I quirked my head to the side, giving prodding nods toward his memory, and gave him a look that said he'd better recall.

"Wait, you're telling me that hot blonde, owns a ranch? The ranch your--." I leaned across the table to slap him gently. "Hey!"

"Yes, Mac is the hot blonde. But the point is: she is also my client. Her brother, Jack, died a few months ago. I told you about him and the article I read before I left. Seems he'd been haunting her house and the bungalow. It used to be a bunkhouse. Mac sensed him in the stables too, of course. And yesterday..." I paused dramatically, "I used my creation to ferret him out, and when he was gone, I spritzed again to make sure of it. Et voila! Ghost begone!"

Chapter Seven

I an was silent.

"Say something. Anything," I reached for his hand and he jerked it back ever so slightly. If I hadn't been watching, I may never have seen that instinctual twitch.

"Do you—" my cellphone buzzed. "Sorry, I have to take this. It's Mac." Mouthing the words, *'the hot blonde,'* I answered. "Hi Mac! What's up?"

"Fiona, can you please return to the ranch? There has been a... disturbance. In the bungalow." My face fell and my heart beat faster. I was a cacophony of emotions.

"What happened?"

"Um, you need to come see this." Mac paused. "There is serious damage to the bungalow. We need to talk." *Crap!* I don't care who you are. Anyone that says 'we need to talk' is about to open a can of worms blindsided by a storm. Ian caught my eye, his brow furrowed in worry, and I fought to keep a somber face considering Mac's accusations, implied and otherwise. But through it all, the odd light in the tunnel was that maybe, just maybe, Spectressence didn't work quite as well as I'd hoped. Which meant, of course, that Jack was still here.

Since we'd walked into town, it took us a while to get back to the ranch. I was not ready for the dragon that was Maisy Catherine Wright.

"Fiona Perry!" Mac bellowed as we crossed the top of the hill. "Meet me. In the. Bungalow." Her command hissed through clenched teeth and it somehow made me feel both that I'd disappointed my mother and that I was being sent to the principal's office. Legs made of lead moved me unsteadily toward the bungalow, and that's when I saw why she was so upset.

"Oh my god, Mac. I am so sorry," I whispered. "I-I-I don't know what happened," I stammered as I took in the scene before me. A shattered floor-to-ceiling window. As we stepped inside, we could see holes punched in nearly every wall. Drawers and tables upended. Knives driven into the kitchen wall in the shape of an upside-down horseshoe—all the luck run out. Broken lamps, pictures stripped from the walls, and ripped up pieces of the newly refinished floor in the living room. Did ghosts have this much... strength? Power? For once in my desire to see and talk to ghosts, I was terrified. What would have happened if we'd been here, or Ian by himself? My frustration with Ian was palpable, but I didn't want him to be hurt.

"Fiona!" Ian's astonished gasp as he came to stand beside me echoed my own feelings.

"I'm okay, Ian." I put my hand on his arm, and turned to Mac. "I am so sorry; I don't know what happened."

"I'll tell you what happened. Your concoction didn't work! That's what happened." Mac stepped closer to me until we were toe-to-toe. "I am not paying you one red cent. You're lucky I don't kick you out right now." She looked at the damage and turned back to me with a sneer. "You made this bed; you can lie in it. Or you can get out and find a hotel. I don't really care, one way or the other."

I felt empathy. The damage had shaken her, and I'd been announcing my success for two days, which was now an utter failure.

"You can't stay here, tonight, Fiona. We can't—the place is a mess. The bedroom has no window..." Ian's voice trailed off as he followed the damage throughout the house. I'd gone into the kitchen to retrieve the kitchen knives from the wall and try to get some semblance of order in the bungalow. The destruction shattered my home, my oasis. But why? I had to get Ian away because if my gut was right and Jack was still around, I needed to talk to him. Find out what had made him lash out. Did he throw these destructive temper tantrums when he was alive too? I'd have to ask Mac. Or not. I was pretty sure she was no longer speaking with me. I had to make things right. But first I had to find out *why*.

"Ian, this is my business. My place. I belong here. But I think you should go." He glanced up at me as he set another lamp upright and began to rehang some pictures that still had wall hooks in the walls.

He cleared his throat. "I don't think that's a good idea..." Mismatched eyes caught mine and bade me look around the place with him. "You may be in danger. What if the vandals come back?"

"Vandals?"

"Who else would do this?" He asked, worried. I pursed my lips wanting to tell him what I thought. But I knew it wouldn't register. Who would believe a ghost had done all this damage? Could do all this damage. Just like he couldn't register ghosts might exist; I couldn't process vandals had done this. I had to talk to Jack. Though secretly thrilled he wasn't gone, it ticked me off about how he'd chosen to let me know he was still here. This was definitely a message for me. But why destroy my bungalow? Or rather, Mac's bungalow, rented by me.

I shrugged. "I don't know, but this is my mess, and I need to clean it up." I looked around. "Literally."

"What will you do for money? I heard Mac say she wouldn't pay you..."

"Maybe not. But I'm a big girl, Ian. I can take care of myself." I walked to where he was standing and hugged him. "Thank you for coming, listening. Even if you can't process what's going on. But I need to be alone now. Do you understand?"

"No. But I'll give you your space. There's a little B&B I passed on my way here. It's not too far." I squeezed his hands. "Thank you."

"Meet me for breakfast tomorrow before I head back to the city?" He asked, hopefully.

"Sure." A quick squeeze, light kiss, and Ian was back in his car heading for the B&B down the road; *Riversong B&B.* I'd passed it plenty on my walks to the river. One more quarter mile and Mac could have claimed it as hers.

* * *

"Jack Wright! Where the hell are you?" He had to be nearby. I felt anger, frustration, and something else I couldn't put a name to. "You realize I LIVE here, right? And I will continue to do so, even if I have to put a blanket over the bedroom window. Thanks for that. You realize it's autumn, right? What, you want me to die from a chill in the air and join you? Well, think again!" Speaking as loudly as I dared, I tried to call a ghost. He didn't answer. But I knew he was watching, and I swear I thought I heard him chuckle.

"Are you *laughing?*" My voice hit an octave of which I didn't know I was capable.

"I was right. You are a spitfire." It was Jack's voice but I couldn't see him.

"Why can't I see you?"

"Because I don't want you to." Was he pouting? It had that ring to it.

"Will you stop acting like a child?"

"I am no child," he said. Jack's voice still sounded as if he were pouting. I rolled my eyes.

"Oh really? How many adults do you know throw temper tantrums and destroy things their sister has worked so hard to build? And in your memory, by the way!" Mac had every right to be angry with me for what Jack had done, but what had I done to make him angry?

Jack's voice softened, "You sound like you still like her. After what she said to you."

"I do still like her, Jack. She's a client because of you. But I'm a friend because of her. She took me in when I needed someone to believe without questions, just acceptance. She's someone I can talk to about anything. Your sister has a good heart, and that's why she's so upset. This bungalow is a tribute to you. Don't you get it?"

"I didn't know that," he said, and his silvery form appeared, hat in hand, his head bowed.

"Well, now you know." I stepped closer, my pulse quickening. "Now that you're here, will you please tell me what caused all... this?" I waved my hand around the room, indicating the damage.

"No." Just as quickly as he'd appeared, he was gone.

Jack's appearance, reappearance, and disappearance in the matter of a few minutes were a mirror to my own emotions on the whole experiment. A fluttering of images, emotions, and in the distance a feeling that something wasn't right. I'd missed something along the way, or maybe I'd gained it but didn't know what to do with it. For a second, I'd thought my gift, or power, as some might have called it, had rules. Scientists need rules. Parameters to follow. But when you're dealing the spirits of the dead, there are no rules.

Chapter Eight

Sleep was a microcosm of chill and strange dreams, but when I woke the sun was up, and I was late. I'd promised to meet Ian for breakfast. As I dressed, I thought about our evening out, wondering what he'd wanted to talk about before Mac had called. He hadn't seen Jack. That much I knew, but Ian had to have felt Jack. His anger in the bungalow had been palpable.

Thankful for another sunny day, I put on a long lavender dress, my denim jacket, and sneakers for the walk toward town. Should I take the car? I briefly waffled between expedience and peace. I chose the latter. No, a walk will be good, a chance to clear my mind and enjoy the fresh air. There was a lot to process and work out.

If Spectressence hadn't worked as I'd thought, what could have gone wrong? Had I missed an ingredient? Should I have covered the solarium more fully, or spritzed all the rooms as I returned to the kitchen? Lost in thought, Ian surprised me. "Good morning, Fiona!" I looked around for the face to match the voice. "Over here." He waved from a bistro table tucked away behind some potted palms.

"Good morning, Ian," I said, making my way to the table. "How did you sleep?" I asked, settling into the chair opposite. He'd already offered coffee, and signaled for the server to bring me a cup. Without asking. Frowning slightly, I shrugged. I had enough battles. I could let the slight slide. Okay, I know he thought he was being gentlemanly or something but come on. I can order for myself, thank you.

"I slept like a log, thanks." He looked around and added, "There really isn't anything like this in Sacramento, is there? There's a buzz in the air during the day here, but late at night, it's like a ghost town." Did he mean to sound... I don't know. Condescending was the first word that came to mind. Ian had a terrible habit of saying whatever was on his mind without thinking about the listener. I wondered if that's why he was a better professor than boyfriend. In class, his delivery was direct, and students accepted his words at face value, but in the nuances of relationships, that same inclination didn't carry over so well. I smiled wanly and hid it in the cup of coffee the server had just brought as I took a sip.

"Now you see what drew me out here."

"I thought a 'ghost' brought you out here," he said, making air quotes as he spoke the word ghost.

Here we go. "You're not wrong. But maybe I should rephrase. What you experienced last night. Here at the B&B," I added knowing his first thoughts would go to the before and after of his time at the bungalow with me. "That's what's keeping me here. This is where I plan to start my business. Yes, a ghost brought me here. But the town itself makes me want to stay. I feel... needed." I hadn't been able to verbalize what had captured my attention to this place until Ian's dig seemed to belittle both the town and me.

"But I need you," He reached across the table, and took my hand. "Come back to the city with me."

So that's why you finagled an invitation! I knew I didn't

remember inviting him. "Is that why you came out here? To ask me to come back to the city with you?" I spoke slowly wanting to ensure he heard and understood the emotions behind the words–shock, anger, frustration, and yes, love. I had loved him, once, and maybe still did, but I had a lot to work out. And I couldn't do it with him here. Or there. "You need me," I repeated, my voice flat.

"I do," he insisted. His eyes caught mine, and a smile played at the corners of his mouth. "And I have some good news. For you."

"For me." I felt an odd sense in my stomach as if the butterflies had stopped moving and formed a baseball. Do not try to 'fix' me, my thoughts shouted at him. I kept my mouth shut.

"Yeah. I talked to the powers that be at the university, and they agreed the explosion was simply an accident. Plus, you've switched to agriculture, like me, anyway, and well," he looked down at our hands still clasped, then back up at me, "there's an opening next semester for a professor. I suggested you." Ian was beaming convinced I'd jump at the chance. And maybe I would have once. In another life.

"No, Ian." I extracted my hands from his and brought them into a near prayer position in front of me. I looked around. "This is where I belong. Yes, Jack brought me here. But I've made friends here, too. Mac being one of the best."

"Mac hates you," Ian said propping his arms on the table.

"No, she was just upset. I get it. I am, too, and would have been if I were in her shoes."

"Ghost healing is not a business, Fiona. It's not... economically viable."

"What? You think there aren't enough ghosts in this town? I can *feel* them, Ian. All around me."

"Can you see them?" He asked.

"Not yet." I paused. "Well, I have once or twice now, but

I'm working the kinks out to make it more permanent." I looked at him pointedly. "To make myself more useful for this business."

"Aargh!" He stretched himself from the table arching his back, his eyes rolling heavenward. "For the last time, Fiona, repeat after me. There is no such thing as ghosts."

"I won't do that, and you know it. I know what I know. Deal with it." I stood up quickly scraping the chair back into another customer. "Sorry," I said without thinking, and showed surprise when Ian asked, "Who are you talking to?"

"What?" I looked behind me. Ian was right. The chair I'd hit was unoccupied, but for the briefest moment I'd seen a woman sitting in it. She was in her late 60s or early 70s wearing clothing that looked like it might have belonged in the 1940s. It was the smoke from her long cigarette that caused me to register someone behind me. They had banned smoking in this little town for over twenty years.

Ian stood up, his hands on the table, and leaned toward me. "Fiona, honey. You need help. You just apologized to a chair." Balancing his weight on one hand, he reached for mine with the other. I left it wanting and almost laughed as he pleaded. "Please, Fi. For me. Come back to the city."

"What part of no is unclear?" I asked, my voice and temperature rising. "Ian, listen to me. I loved university life. Past tense. But I've found something here that you can't measure in a beaker, or calculate the numbers, or quantify or qualify. It belies all logic and is what keeps me here. It's the chance to trace the unknown and maybe learn something different along the way. I'm tired of measuring my life. I'm not sowing wild oats. The work contains elements of science, but without so many constraints, to allow for the odd occurrence you can't write about but understand at a soul level. Understand?"

"No, I don't. I never did. If I can't see, smell, touch, or

taste it, I can't believe in it." He shrugged and added, "Or those who do. It was a mistake to come here." Placing a few bills on the table, he strode toward his car, got in and drove off without another word.

Ian's words stung more than I cared to admit, but I would not follow the rules. I'd meant what I'd said. I felt needed here, and while Mac was upset, she'd get over it. Especially once I went back to the drawing board to see what the hell had gone wrong with my formula. First, I had to get Ian out of my head. I doubted myself plenty. I didn't need his help. If I could get him to believe me, to see what I knew, then he'd understand. He had to. Just as quickly as those thoughts formed, another came to mind. Why do you care so much what Ian thinks?

The answer came quickly. Because you have something to prove and you won't rest until you can. "Right. I don't care what it takes." There was only one problem. Ian wouldn't return my calls.

Chapter Nine

Two weeks later, I had a missed call from Ian. Good. Anger and frustration had been building, but without the object of my wrath in front of me, I was pretty stoic. I huffed when I saw the blinking ID and the time. He'd returned my call in the middle of the day when he'd knew I'd likely be on one of my daily walks. Which is most of what I'd been doing these last couple of weeks, anyway.

Mac was only speaking to me for concerns related to business. The ranch business, and our development of the new feed product. Not a word about Jack, no dropping by for a glass of wine, and no invites to the ranch house. I was thankful she'd at least gotten workers started on the bungalow to repair the damage.

Returning Ian's call later that night, I wondered if Jack would appear. But then, I hadn't seen him in those two weeks either, and I couldn't go back to the solarium to check. Though I thought I'd seen a form inside one day when returning for a walk. Turned out later, it was Mac getting spices from the wall hanging planters for a dinner she was hosting for her group of small business owners in the area. But just because he chose not to show himself, didn't mean he wasn't there. I could still feel his anger permeating from the walls, and even a little in the air on my walks down to the river.

"Ian," I said when he picked up, and stopped. What was I supposed to say next? *I need you to believe in ghosts to prove you believe in me*, my inner voice raising the statement into a question. That sounded ridiculous, but I knew there was some truth to it.

"What Fiona? What do you want?" He sounded upset. Sad. But I could still hear the undercurrent of disdain. He couldn't wrap his mind around it. What I did, what I wanted to do with my life – to speak to the dead. It was completely illogical, and if I'd been in his shoes, I might have thought the same. All I wanted was for him to step into mine.

"I want you to believe—"

"I don't believe in Santa Claus or the Tooth Fairy, either. So, it's not just you." His tone was biting, but I couldn't give up. Not yet. If I could convince Dr. Ian Quigley, a biochemist with a professorship at Cal State, then there'd be no question I could do this. Take up the reins of this role I'd been, what, gifted? Cursed? Whatever it was, it was part of me now.

"Okay, then. I'll show you. Come to Coloma this weekend." Ian chuffed on the other line like a tiger, and I wondered if he knew. I knew it as his 'fine I'll do it but don't want to' exhale burst, and wondered why he was so quick to give in.

"I'm busy this weekend," he said, thinking of a way to say no, I imagined. "But I can come out Sunday night and stay through Monday, it's a school holiday." Ian was silent as he waited for me to comment. I didn't take the bait.

"See you Sunday, Ian," I said and hung up the phone.

A few days later, Ian arrived. He looked different. His skin was pasty as if he hadn't been in the sun much and his eyes seemed to stare at nothing and everything all at once. "Are you okay?" I asked opening the door for him to come in.

"Fine. Let's do this. Show me what you want me to see." He sat down on the newly upholstered couch and sank into it his arms extended on either side as if to embrace the back of it.

I turned toward the kitchen for my vial of Spectressence and breathed deeply. Breath in. Breath out. You're on kid, I thought as I picked up the vial and turned back toward the living room. Shoving it at him like the perfume girl in a mall, I jumped as he recoiled. "Relax," I said to myself and to him. "This doesn't turn you into a ghost. It turns a ghost into a form we can see. This is for Jack. Not you."

He laughed. "You're on the first name basis with a ghost?" Ian asked with emphasis on the word ghost, his face flush with–I don't know–surprise, maybe?

"Ghosts may be dead. But they are—were—people, you know." Frowning, I narrowed my eyes and hoped he felt like he was a bug under a microscope.

"Sorry!" He held up his hand. "I won't disparage your ghost. Now how does that thing work?" He asked, pointing at the vial.

"Well, it's not rocket science. Simply point and spritz." I demonstrated hoping Jack might appear. No such luck.

"Is it working?" Ian asked looking around the room. He sniffed. "It smells good. You could always sell it as a perfume if it doesn't work as..." his eyes rolled to the right thinking. "Ghost Reveal," he finished, cupping his hands and spreading them apart as he said the word reveal. He was making fun, and Jack wasn't helping. Where had he gone?

When no one was talking to me, I'd had plenty of time to go back to the drawing board. I'd bought new equipment in case I had compromised the old equipment. I recalculated every equation, run every number, every scenario, and got the same answer. Spectressence worked. Except it didn't. Wouldn't. Couldn't? Had I rechecked its Ph levels? Check.

Had I confirmed a plastic vial with a spray cap wouldn't dilute its efficacy? Check. So, where was Jack?

"Fiona," Ian said my name so softly I almost didn't hear him. I was fighting back tears at the stress of my life's work not working, and facing hard facts about my future. Ian took my hands in his and drew me close, then pulled me down until my calves were on his thighs, then he kissed me, but not passionately. It was paternal and delivered at my forehead rather than my lips. "It doesn't work, Fi. You need to admit that now. Not to me, but to yourself."

A Thomas Edison quote came to mind. The one about his answer to a question of failure. He says, "I did not fail. I learned 2,000 or 10,000 times, (I forget how many) how not to make a light bulb." Words in parentheses are mine.

Suddenly, I laughed, first a burbly giggle and soon a full-blown belly laugh. I couldn't stop, and the look in Ian's eyes made me laugh even harder. I can't overstate what a relief it was to laugh.

"I have been ghosted. By a ghost!" I went on howling like a banshee at my realization, but as I came down off the strange high of it, the questioning look in Ian's eyes drove me to explain. I filled Ian in on the rest. "I've tried everything. I scrapped all my notes and started from scratch. I visited all the places where I sensed him before, and the place where I'd proved, or thought I'd proved my theory: the solarium. But then, I figured the place I'd felt him most strongly was here, and thought if I brought you back—"

"Wait a minute." Ian let go, and I clattered to the floor. "Was I bait? For a ghost?"

"Well, I hadn't thought of it that way, but I guess you were in a way." I scrunched my hands into the braided rug and pulled myself up. Dusting myself off, I stood up to my full height in an effort to match his, and put my hands on my hips. "Would you have come if I hadn't? I called after you left me at the B&B's café, and not a word until two weeks later. I need someone on my side. I'd hoped it might be you." Dropping my arms to my sides, I shrugged, palms up. "Guess I was wrong."

"Stop making me the bad guy here. You've known how I felt about this since we've known each other. I haven't changed." Ian frowned. "Besides, even if you could prove it, what are the odds I'd even believe it. Even if I saw it with my own eyes. I'd still be looking for that trick of the light, trick of the imagination, whatever you want to call it. What I want to know is, why are you trying so hard for this guy? Aren't there other ghosts you could show me, or is he your one hit wonder?"

I didn't have an answer for him. He was right, surely there were other ghosts. But this was the one I felt... closest to in some strange way. The look in Ian's eyes as they bore into mine were unstinting, cold. Then they softened as he continued, "Listen, Fi. I don't want to fight. But are you in love with him? This ghost of yours." I quirked my mouth and looked down, studying my toes as if they had the answer.

My mind shouted, "Yes!" But I shook my head, and said, "It's not that. I don't know what it is. Yet. But until I figure it out..."

"There's not a place for me in your life," Ian finished. I nodded and could feel my eyes tearing up a little, but none would shed. Taking my hands in his, he caressed the inside of my wrists. "I don't understand any of this, and I think you're crazy for choosing a ghost over a living, breathing man. But," he paused, and I knew the next words took some effort. "I'll leave you alone to let you figure things out. I don't like it. But I enjoy sharing you with a dead guy less." Without another word, he was gone. Back to his university life.

Giving me space had been hard for him, and I loved him for it. Did I still love Ian? I think I did, but it had changed somehow. I couldn't put my finger on it. As I thought about his words and his question, I wondered how I could be in love with two peas in a pod except one was dead and the other wasn't. For anyone else, it would have been a simple decision. Go for the guy who's here. Human. But not me. Not Fiona Perry, ghost healer.

Chapter Ten

Mac's business had been going downhill when I arrived, and it took her a while to tell me the ghost of her dead brother was haunting her. The rentals, the farm experiences, the rides on the horses, and touring walks throughout the acreage had all taken a hit, especially around the ranch house, bungalow, and stables. These are the places Jack frequented the most, she'd explained.

So, I'd gone and opened my big mouth telling her I could heal her haunted home. Man, I'd been cocky. The indigo, lavender, and gray patterned maxi dress with longer sleeves helped to keep the chill out a little. It helped, too, that the builders had been quick, and the damage that Jack had done would soon be a distant memory. What I couldn't, or rather who, I couldn't get out of my head, was what Ian had said before he'd walked out a second time. Why is this one so important? I had no answer then, and I don't have one now. There wasn't rhyme or reason to it other than a feeling. What feeling that was? Another puzzle entirely.

The vial of Spectressence sat on a shelf in the kitchen, and as I looked at it, I remembered how excited I'd been to tell Mac of its success. She'd begun hosting dinner parties again, and was planning events for the coming holidays, into the spring. I'd offered her hope, then snatched it back. My experiment failed; I dialed Mac's number.

"Yes?" Mac never said 'hello' on the phone. "*I don't know why, really. I've always answered it that way. Maybe because I think it will make people get to their point faster*," she'd told me when I'd first moved in, and the stovetop's gas flame kept going out as if someone was blowing it out. I'd called her to ask about getting it fixed. Mac had come herself to repair it saying, "I've gotten pretty good at this, thanks to Jack."

"Mac. It's Fiona." I took a breath. She must not have been looking at the ID. If she had, I don't think she'd have answered. "Thanks for—"

"What do you want, Fiona?" she asked, cutting me off. "I've got to rebook two events, finalize payments to the builders, feed the horses, reschedule several appointments..." I half expected her to say 'etcetera'. There was a long pause as I worked out what to say. I'd dialed before I'd given full thought to it. "In a nutshell," she finished, "I'm busy. So, what do you want?"

"Yes, sorry. I know. I could help you with some of that. Take some of it off your plate."

"You've done enough. And you haven't answered my question," Mac said. She blew a breath out, and I caught the frustration and worry in her voice.

"I need to talk to you. Let me make you dinner." I stopped. "It's the least I could do. Think of it as a thank you, after..." You fool, you've said too much. She just told you she had to finalize payment with the builders. You know, the ones redoing the bungalow you're staying in, that your ghost destroyed while you were out. I went further out on the limb I was on, and added, "Plus, I miss you. You're the only one I really know here." Before I could babble any further on, she answered me.

"Fiona, stop." I pressed my lips together to keep them from moving. "Give someone space to answer your question... well, it wasn't a question, was it?"

"No," I said, sheepishly.

"Dinner's a bit much, though I appreciate the offer. Maybe for now, just a glass of wine? I think we could both use a glass," Mac said. "I've got a lot going on today. But tomorrow works. 6:30pm?"

"I'll be there. Thank you for talking to me. I know you're from the wine country and a wine connoisseur, but let me bring you a bottle. It's the least I can do since you don't want me to make dinner."

"That's fine, Fiona. I'll see you at 6:30 tomorrow evening." Like Ian, she hadn't answered my calls for weeks, so I knew she must be softening. It must have been scary to come home to and see the major damage Jack had caused. But I was glad she answered my call now. I had to clear the air. She was my friend. I liked her and wanted to help her. God knew, I'd tried.

* * *

I watched Mac hang up the phone. She had tears in her eyes, and I had caused them. Me and my temper tantrum at the bungalow. I reached for her shoulder and watched my hand move through it. Mac gave a start and put her hand where mine hand been.

"I'm sorry, Sis," I said. Knowing she couldn't hear me. "You were counting on me, and I let you down. First by dying. Believe me, I wasn't expecting that either. And then, by scaring you. I was scared, too. Had no idea what was happening. Had happened. But you were grieving. Are grieving, and I can't let you let me go. I want to stay here. I want Fiona."

Mac looked around as if she'd heard me. She sighed and went back to the laptop on the kitchen table. Papers. No, not papers. Bills. That's what covered her laptop. She'd lied to Fiona. There was nothing she was rebooking or rescheduling. I glimpsed the Excel sheet she had open. JMC Ranch P&L. She closed the laptop before I could see the bottom line. But she remained at the table with her head in her hands.

* * *

"Thanks for agreeing to meet me tonight, Mac," I said, pouring from the bottle I'd just opened. "I wanted to talk to you about what happened last month. You know there's only one person it could have been."

Mac nodded. "I had my suspicions. But that's not why I was upset."

"It's not?" I asked, surprised. "Why were you upset?"

"It had already been a pretty rough day, and when I got back. Well, the destruction was just too much."

"I see. Well, that's what I want to talk about." Mac's face didn't change expression. She wasn't angry or upset. Just impassive. "I made you a promise and didn't deliver. When you came home and I'd tried Spectressence in the Solarium, I truly thought it had worked. But it proved me wrong." I waited for Mac to say something. When she didn't, I continued.

"Anyway, I wanted to let you know that I've tried everything. I went through everything again to see if I'd missed anything, and if so, what it could be. There's nothing. From a mathematical and biochemical standpoint, Spectressence is solid. But in application, well that's a different story. It doesn't work. I have proven this beyond any doubt." I waved a hand across the path to the bungalow. Then, I took an envelope from my pocket and handed it to her. "This is for you."

Mac's brows furrowed as she took the envelope but didn't open it. "What is it?"

"It's what I owe you for the damages. It's my fault that happened—"

"How is it your fault?" Mac asked.

"I'm still not sure, other than that I'm renting the bungalow from you, but I feel responsible for it. I don't know what set Jack off that day, but..." I shrugged, raised my hands palms up, and offered a sad smile.

"You still think it was Jack."

"I do," I said, and when I said it out loud, I suddenly understood why he'd been so upset. "Ooohhh..." I said with a knowing nod. Then stopped. I couldn't prove it unless Jack told me. But at least I could set Mac at ease. I knew she needed the money. It's hard to run a ranch business by yourself, and extras like destroyed bungalows that were only recently remodeled put quite the damper on the wallet.

Mac blinked back tears. "Thank you," she whispered. Then wiped them away, and asked, "What now?"

I took a sip of wine and laughed. "I don't know. The money's run out." I'd just given Mac the last of my startup money. Maybe she could pay the builders and start something of her own with the money. "I have no job, no prospects, nothing. But I still feel something pulled me here to this town, to you and JMC Ranch."

"It's called a newspaper article, darlin'," she said with a southern twinge. Where had that come from?

"I suppose you're right. That article spoke to me."

"Did Jack?"

"Did Jack what?"

"Speak to you."

I raised my eyebrows and considered her question. Yes, he'd spoken to me. "Yes, he did," I answered finally.

"He's still here, right? He's not gone." Her voice was flat. Black circles under her eyes gave her usually bright face a despondent look, and I wondered how much longer JMC Ranch might exist. She was at her wit's end, and no one to turn to. Not really. Well, unless you counted the business cooperative, I guess.

"Right..." I leaned closer. "Why do you ask?"

"Because he was here. Earlier. I felt him. His presence." Mac sighed, and exhaling collapsed in on herself. I knew how she felt. But I also knew how strong she was. How strong we both were. So, like any good ranch woman, she lifted her chin and jutted it out in defiance. "I can't take your money, Fiona." She shrugged and thrust the envelope back at me. "It doesn't matter, anyway. This place..." her voice trailed off, her gaze moving from her hands to the floor to me to a huge painting over the fireplace. "It's been here since the beginning..." I followed her gaze. Well, not a painting. It was plans. Plans for the ranch, I assumed. Why they had such a prominent space, I did not know. There was a tension in the room that wasn't anger. It was something else. A deep, deep sadness.

I waved the envelope away. "Keep it. My work here... it's hopeless, Mac. I'm sorry. He doesn't want to be seen now and I think he wants to stay here. He's stuck, and either isn't ready or doesn't want to move on. But as for my Spectressence, I'd have more luck seeing and talking to ghosts if I was that kid from The Sixth Sense. I'm sorry I couldn't heal your home, and for the bungalow," I said, directing her to the still unopened envelope in her hands, I said, "I hope that can cover all the repairs on the bungalow, and that it helps a little against all the other things you've got going on." She glanced at me sharply, and I nodded. I understood more than she realized. We were in the same boat, basically.

"You have no idea," she whispered as if to herself, but I was close enough to hear. Both of us lost in our own thoughts, I got up to leave. "Fiona," her voice cracked against my name. I turned around, and she offered a half smile. I nodded in acknowledgement and headed back across the gravel path to the bungalow.

Chapter Eleven

The phone rang. "Hello?" I hadn't looked at the ID. With a pot of spaghetti sauce simmering, and water boiling for the noodles, I was keeping an eye on the water levels, so nothing boiled over. A split baguette with garlic butter was in the oven toasting. There was a lot to keep track of, and the phone was the least of my concerns. Until I heard his voice.

"Fiona?" It was Ian. I rolled my eyes. We'd left things pretty well closed, I thought, and wondered why he was calling.

"What do you want, Ian?" I asked, my voice sharp with impatience. Looking around the kitchen, I checked on the water for the spaghetti. The slow boil that means it's ready for the pasta, was forming. Holding the phone between my ear and my shoulder, I was hands free to add a little salt and split the hard noodles into two so it would be easier for them to cook. "I'm a little busy right now," I added, hoping he'd either get to the point or get off the phone.

"You're busy? With what?" You piece of—ugh! I checked the garlic bread in the oven.

"Does it matter? The point is for you to get to the point. What do you want?" I said the last question slowly, emphasizing each word, and hoped I sounded as terse as I meant to.

"Sorry!" I could imagine Ian holding up a hand to stop a tongue lashing that would not come. He wouldn't bait me into a fight. Not tonight. "Fiona, I called because I was hoping we could try again. Would you meet me at the *Riversong B&B* for dinner tomorrow night?"

"What?"

"I want to take you to dinner. Seems the *Riversong* is expanding, and they've opened a new restaurant," he explained. "It's a little bistro and dinner only, but they have the most amazing food."

"How do you know about it and I don't?" I demanded. This was my town now, not his. I was on edge already and my instinct was to say 'no.' But then that old nagging voice returned with two simple words. *What If?* I debated silently as I stirred the spaghetti sauce percolating in its pot. It's almost metaphorical—just enough heat to percolate in a pot, and bring to a boil without boiling over. Yep, that's pretty much how I felt.

"Are you there, Fiona? Will you meet me tomorrow? I miss you and want to see you." He sounded almost pleading which was very un-Ian like. Something was off. What did he really want, I wondered? And would he even tell me if I asked? Probably not.

"Give me one good reason I should come. You've made it clear on multiple occasions what you thought of me, and by extension my dreams, passions, and desires for my professional life. There was a time I thought I could come to you for comfort, but I learned the hard way, I was wrong. So, Ian, please. Tell me what I can do for you and you don't even have to buy me dinner! What is it you're after?" My voice rose as I launched into my answer. Which upon reflection was a long-winded 'no.' But did that stop Ian? Nope.

"Okay. Okay. You're busy, I get it. With what I don't know. So, I'll cut to the chase." Finally!

"Go on," I encouraged. "What's this call *really* about?"

"Turns out, I fell in love. With Coloma. Like you. A friend of mine from Sacramento is a restauranteur who was interested in opening a small upscale bistro in a small town as a sort of launching pad. He has an Executive Chef who studied in Paris, but when I told him about your cooking, he asked if you might want the job. If you say yes, he'll move the other guy to one of his other restaurants in the city."

I felt the shock of this news. "So, tomorrow night was...?" I asked a question I already knew the answer to.

"An informal interview. Over dinner."

"So let me get this straight." I began to tick items on my fingers knowing he couldn't see them. I'd finally thought of putting the phone on speaker, so I could be truly hands free, and yet found myself leaning over it to ensure he heard every word.

"One, you've been back in Coloma for how long and didn't tell me you were here? This is a small town with few places to hide, Ian. I should have seen you, if only in passing. Two, you *assumed* I might need and want a job doing something completely different from my training background, that has nothing to do with my years at the university. Why? Because you think I'm crazy? I am no damsel in distress. Please stop treating me as such!" I punched the button to hang up and wished for a handset to slam down onto its cradle.

My blood boiling, I looked at the saucepan with the red sauce aiming for the rim, and the boiling water with the spaghetti. I'd let it cook too long. *Shit!* What was that smell? The garlic bread! The oven smoked, and I pulled out the bread. There was a char on it, but it was still partly edible.

Then, a glint of light from the setting sun on my vial of Spectressence, and I lost complete control.

Grabbing the vial, I held it over my head and dashed it to the floor. The glass splintered into a thousand pieces that looked like diamonds on the floor in the fading light. "A lifetime of lies! Believing I could do something that is.... impossible. I'd proven it not once, but twice." A red mist filled my vision as the anger and frustration boiled over and I stood immobile, my emotions vying for top place. I'd just destroyed everything I'd worked for in a fit of rage. I had no money. No place to stay. My rent was up at the end of the week. And then I smelled it.

An overwhelming peppermint smell that gave me a headache but bade me close my eyes, anyway. I'd get used to the smell soon enough, I reasoned. The liquid of Spectressence puddled at my feet began to spread and evaporate. At least, I thought it was evaporating. Then the puddle gathered and rose. In vapor form, it swirled around me. I breathed deeply and the sharpness of the peppermint entered my nose cavity. I could taste it on my tongue. It felt like hours but had been only seconds, and when I looked down at the shattered glass, no liquid remained. I'd absorbed every drop into myself. It was a heady sensation, but my mind was clearer, sharper than it had ever been.

What did this accident mean? I had no idea. But at least it hadn't caused a fire like at the lab. I couldn't afford it. Figuratively and literally. Regardless, something had changed. I'd added peppermint oil just a drop or two at the very last second when concocting Spectressence. It was supposed to enhance communication, and particularly good for those with a focus in mediumship. I was no medium, but I'd figured it was the closest to what I wanted to do.

In my world, ghosts appear when they want to. Not when I ask them. I looked down at my arms, and they glistened.

Checking the mirror, every bit of me looked, well, wet, for lack of a better term. Which I guess stood to reason, but there's no way there was enough liquid in the vial to cover an entire body. Had it expanded when it had the air it needed? I'd have to double check that to prove it. The peppermint caught in my throat, and for a second I thought it was trying to choke me from the inside. But the sensation receded, and I breathed easier.

Knock! Knock! "Fiona, are you in there?" It was Mac. "I was walking by and thought I heard a crash. Are you okay?"

"I'm fine, Mac. Door's open!" I was beaming. I'd never felt so good. The sky was brighter when she opened the door and there was a light buzzing sound in my ear, but it wasn't distressing. It felt almost like someone singing.

Mac stepped inside tentatively, then her jaw dropped. "Wow! Look at you. You're glowing." She half-whispered the last, and covered her mouth with her hand. "You're not—" She began dropping her hand to her side again.

I laughed. "No! It's not that. It's just, I don't know," I waved a hand toward the still open doorway. "Such a beautiful day. I'm just giddy with it."

"Okay..." Mac's eyes narrowed. "Have you looked in the mirror? You look stunning, but there's something else too, that I can't place." A shadow crossed my face for a second and I went to the full-length mirror in the bedroom walk-in closet. Then I saw what she saw.

Mac wasn't kidding when she said I was glowing. My skin had a transparent sheen wrapped around it. Protecting it. My eyes were wider, brighter. Fingers seemed elongated, then they retracted to their normal size. My red hair wasn't a composite of mahogany and red as before, now it was a deep red, almost purple, which gave my glowing skin an odd bluish tinge to it. Would it go away, I wondered? And why could Mac see it?

Palm meet forehead. Because she's a Sensitive and doesn't

know it. How else would she have been able to sense Jack's presence? Plus, she'd accepted my claims at face value I could heal haunted houses. No skepticism. Just acceptance. There was definitely something more to Mac than met the eye. She'd tell me in her own time.

"Uh, Fiona?" Mac called out, and I could hear the clatter of glass. Everything had happened so fast I hadn't cleaned up yet. Uh-oh. "Can you come here a second?"

"Be right there!" I answered, taking a last look in the mirror. The bright glow was fading. Was it going away, or going deeper in? I wasn't sure and wondered how I'd be able to tell. I entered the kitchen and saw Mac with the hand-held brush broom and dustpan sweeping up the shattered glass.

"You'll need to be careful in here. I'm trying to get all the glass swept up." She looked up at me. "I thought you'd switched to a plastic bottle with a sprayer. What changed?" She asked.

"I switched it because the plastic may have been diluting the efficacy of Spectressence after all, so I put it back in the glass vial."

"I see. Did it work?" When I didn't answer, she rephrased it for my questioning look. "Did putting Spectressence back in the glass vial work? Or is it like trying to put the genie back in the bottle?"

"Oh." I quirked my mouth. "I guess we'll never know," I said spreading my hands across the space where I'd broken the bottle. "Sorry I've caused you so much trouble. I know my rent is up end of the week. Now we're at the end of this month..."

"You're my only customer. You can stay longer if you need to."

"Actually, I can't. I'll have to go home. The money I gave you for repairs—" I smiled weakly and shrugged.

"Was the last of your startup money. Your savings," Mac

finished, so I wouldn't have to. She dropped her eyes, her shoulders slumped. She took a deep breath, then raised her head and put her shoulders back. Instinctively, I did the same. "Well, I guess we're both in a pickle then, aren't we? Let's be in this pickle together. We'll work something out for your rent, and you can stay here as long as you need to."

"Thanks, Mac. You're a good friend. I appreciate it, but it seems I have some kinks to work out in the city..."

"You mean that Dr. Ian guy? He can work himself out. Good riddance, I say." She stopped and looked at me closely. "It is good riddance, right?" I smiled but didn't motion in agreement. I was still on the fence, even after everything he'd said and done.

"You're looking more like yourself now," she said, changing the topic. "That intense glow you had was kinda freaking me out." Mac laughed, her old belly laugh. I did, too. And felt even better when she added, "Listen, I'm going to be away for a day or so taking care of some things. Would you mind keeping an eye on the place? You don't have to do anything. There are no customers or visitors, and the staff is a skeleton crew, here to feed the horses and do general upkeep."

"I'd be happy to, Mac. Thank you for your trust in me."

Chapter Twelve

I t had been a strange few days since Mac left. On my daily walks to the river, the trees seemed brighter, their harvest leaves punched up, as if digitally enhanced. The river's burbling was louder, and I was beginning to understand it. I could see the energy of the landscape, that near invisible white shimmering where you know there must be something on the other side. And if you concentrate hard enough, you'll gain access to the backstage of the world.

The ranch house was quiet when I went inside. I looked in toward the solarium, but made no move to go there. I couldn't go in there. Not yet. Maybe best if I don't go in at all, I cautioned myself. Instead, I took a magazine from the coffee table and sat down on the couch across from the fireplace. Embers from another night had long died down, and the ashes swept from below the grate. I had stacked fresh logs neatly in the tin, and thought about starting a fire. I canceled the thought just as quickly.

My volatility was perilous; echoes of the near destruction of the bungalow giving me pause. I wasn't reading the magazine, only idly flipping through its pages. A sense of nervous excitement pervaded my senses, and the old familiar tingling sensation in my toes made itself known. Jack. He was here. Somewhere.

I jumped. What was that? Footsteps? I was the only one in the house; I knew. So, I stood up and called out. "Who's there?" No answer. I picked up a fire poker from the cold fireplace, wielding it like a sword. Walking down the hallway, all the doors were closed except one. The solarium. My feet moved faster. I strode into the solarium, and straight into his arms. "Jack!" He was solid, as if alive. Real. My heart raced, trying desperately to break free of my chest.

"Whoa," Jack began. "You were a vision before, but..." he took a step back and eyed me from head-to-toe, drinking in the image. "There's something different about you."

"There's something different about you, too." I squeezed his upper arm. "How are you," I paused wondering how to ask. "Here? Like this, I mean."

He laughed. "I'm not really sure. But I am here. Real. Human." He pinched himself. "Yep, no ghosts here." Jack pulled me to him and his mouth found mine. The warmth of his lips surprised me. He kissed me again with lips both soft and strong. I don't know what I thought they'd have been like, but this was uncharted territory. "I have been wanting to do that properly for so long."

Then Jack did something completely unexpected. He sniffed me. "What are you doing?" I asked, laughing. Taking a step back I watched his expression change. For just a second, a shadow flickered. Soon he was smiling again and laughing.

"There are things I want to do, too," he said, lowering his eyes and tracing the scoop neckline on my dress.

"What was that face?" I asked, letting him continue to trace the shape of a wide u from clavicle to clavicle. I shivered at this touch. But now that I could see and talk to him, I had questions. I'm a scientist. We ask questions.

Jack pouted, moving his index finger down and drawing a light circle around first one breast, then the other. "I don't want to answer questions. I want you. Whatever that scent is you're wearing is intoxicating, and it's making me hot."

I took his hands in mine and moved them to my hips. "What do you smell, Jack?"

"Peppermint," he said, his breath quickening. Ah, now I knew how to get him to answer my questions.

Wrapping his arms around me, I stepped closer until there was no space between our bodies. "Why are you here, Jack? What's keeping you on the ranch?"

"I have to help Maisy. Mac. I have to protect her." He bent his head and laid it on my chest, his silky dark hair tickling my skin. "She's my sister. I shouldn't have left." Left?

"Jack, you didn't leave. You died. You know that, right?" I explained. Was he one of those spirits who simply didn't know they were dead? I thought about unbuttoning his shirt, and as I did so, his shirt opened as if I'd done it. Well, this was new. He stepped back, a half-smile on his lips, and mischief in his eyes.

"You're glowing. Did you know that?" He asked. "Am I doing that?"

"No. At least I don't think so." Warmth spread its cover from my shoulders and down my legs, leaving its imprint just below my belly button. Jack grabbed me then, holding me against him.

"It's the peppermint," he explained. "I don't have any control. I can't... stop." We'd both begun to glow and glisten as if sweating, and had done nothing more than kiss and touch each other. But it seemed Spectressence created arousal on both sides of the veil.

Ignoring his confession, I continued, lowering my hand to his zipper. His breath caught, and I stopped short. "Jack, you need to leave this place. This isn't your home anymore. Mac knows you wanted to help." Something tugged at my brain. "When you said 'shouldn't have left', what did you mean?"

"Not dead, left. Left, left. Mac and I had a fight the night I died. I was angry about something. I can't remember what it was now. Only that I was angry. Punching walls. Kicking dirt. Tantrum stuff." He gasped as I stepped out of my dress and moved toward the chaise.

"Come," I said. I wanted him to tell me more about what had happened. But I wanted him with every fiber of my being even more. My toes curled as he ambled toward me. I pulled him down to meet my eyes and kissed him. "And you upset one of the horses," I finished, assuming the truth. He shook his head.

"No, I hurt Mac's horse, and it responded in kind. It's like the horse knew I was mad at Mac, but didn't expect the result when it kicked me."

"Mmm... you didn't expect the result either," I said, tracing my finger down the center of his chest. "So, how can you best help Mac as a ghost? Is there anything you want me to say to her for you?"

"I'll tell you later. Right now, I have other plans," his words fading as he covered my mouth with his, and wrapped me around him. We sunk from the chaise to the floor in the solarium, and surrounded by plants and herbs, an indoor oasis, we came together as one.

Spent, we lay in each other's arms, still exploring each other's bodies. "Wow. That was...."

"Yes, it was," Jack said. His deep baritone with the hint of the south finished the conversation we'd started. "I owe you some answers. Or one, anyway." I nodded, deep in concentration on his body, tracing the lines of him. "You asked me how I could help Mac as a ghost? I can't." He shrugged. "I thought I could, but all I'm doing is driving her crazy and wrecking the only thing she has left of the Wright family. This ranch. Everyone. Everything else is gone." He looked at me. "I think that's why she found a friend in you. I'm sorry about the bungalow."

"The bungalow?"

"I thought for sure you'd suspected. Maybe even knew."

"Well, I knew it was you. Of course. What I don't know is why." I rolled onto my side and caught his eye. Jack looked away. He quirked his mouth and replied, "I was jealous."

"Of what? Who—Oh, I see." I don't know why I hadn't seen it before. Ian and I had made love the same day I'd had the sensual encounter with Jack.

"He's not right for you, you know," Jack said, breaking into my thoughts.

"And you are?"

"Well, yeah. Or at least, I would be if I was alive." He laughed. "I'd stick around for you and leave Mac alone," Jack teased.

"It doesn't work that way, Jack, and you know it."

"Just think, you could say you were dating Mr. Wright. I could be your imaginary boyfriend, except..." Jack stopped, and his hand that had been caressing my wrist turned ethereal, dropping mine.

"Good, you see the flaw in your theory." Frowning, I worried my lip, the wheels turning in my mind. "What happened before? When you weren't solid. When I sprayed Spectressence..."

"Is that what you call it?" Jack started to laugh, then stopped. "Sorry, but it sounds like a perfume."

I smiled. "That's what Mac said. You two were peas in a pod, weren't you? But you didn't answer my question. I thought you'd gone, and then when you destroyed the bungalow, I knew it hadn't worked. Though I'd announced that it did to your sister."

"It worked. For a few minutes. But I guess it wasn't very long lasting or something. I'm sorry."

"For what? It's not your fault," I said kissing him softly.

"I've caused a lot of trouble by sticking around, haven't I?" Jack said, his voice low.

"You didn't mean to. Plus, you were angry. Are you still?"

"Am I still what?"

"Angry."

"No."

"Then, you're ready."

"For what?" Jack rolled over to face me, his eyes sparkling.

"To go to the other side. Into the light or something. There's another place for you. A better place."

"How do you know?"

"I don't, but I trust the process. And I have seen the face of someone who knew. That was all I needed to believe."

"You lost someone?"

"Yes. A long time ago. They came back for a few minutes, but only to say goodbye. I didn't learn until a few days later that they hadn't come back. I'd been communing with a ghost. You're the first ghost, solid though you are, I've been able to talk to and touch."

"You have definitely touched me." He pointed to different parts of his body. "Here and here and here and... I could go on."

"Yes, I imagine you could. So, you still haven't answered my two most important questions. Is there anything you want me to tell Mac for you? And are you ready to enter the next phase, plane, I'm not sure what to call it, but I know you'll be happy there."

Jack closed his eyes. I felt a heaviness leave me I hadn't realized was there. "Do you feel like you're floating on a cloud?" he asked.

"Yes."

"Me, too." He smiled and mimed taking a picture. "Something to remember you by. And yes, I'm ready. But I want to talk to Mac through you, if I can. Do you know how long this Spectressence stuff lasts now that you're it?"

"What do you mean, I'm it?"

"I mean, you spilled it and it's infused into you. You are your creation."

"Oh, wow."

"Wow, is right. Why do I suddenly feel like someone's turned the hourglass over?" He pointed to his solid form. "In case this doesn't last. This is what I want you to tell Mac from me." He whispered it in my ear, making the back of my neck tingle, and I hoped I could remember it. Then, he looked over my shoulder. "I see it. I see where I'm supposed to go now. Don't forget what I said and tell Mac. It's important."

Chapter Thirteen

"Hey, Fiona! I'm--! Jack?" Mac burst into the house two days earlier than expected and saw her brother again. In his birthday suit, and me in mine. Once I shook the cobwebs from my brain, and my deer-in-the-headlights look resolved, I searched frantically for something to cover myself. I was at my client's *house!* Naked. With her dead brother. Anyone else would have fainted on the spot.

Jack turned to smile at her and waved. "She can't hear me, can she?"

"No," I whispered out the side of mouth. "But she can see you, so... cover up." I tossed his jeans at him. He laughed, and I rolled my eyes. "This is not funny, Jack."

"It is from where I'm standing. Sitting. Laying," he corrected himself until he landed on the right word. "Now, I really wish I could stay."

"You can't. It's time for you to move on, so that she can move on," I waved a hand toward Mac.

Frozen in place, Mac whispered, "Jack?" He nodded. "He can hear me?" She turned to me for confirmation.

"Yes, but I'm not sure why. I'm surprised you can see him." She laughed.

"Well, seeing him with you makes a lot more sense than me seeing you alone and naked in the solarium."

"Good point." I'd been redressing as she spoke, and felt a bit more confident being covered. Jack's voice made me turn my head. It was like the first time, when he sounded as if he was at the other end of a tunnel. He dressed again, too. Complete with hat in hand. At least he had the sense to look sheepish.

A single wave of energy flowed through my veins, and I realized it was Jack saying goodbye. He shimmered like the silver photo negative of himself when we first met. Then he was gone. Mac turned to me, still shaking her head in shock and disbelief.

"That *was* Jack, right? How did he--? How could I--?" She looked at me, her eyes asking questions I couldn't answer.

"I don't know. But he's gone, Mac. For good this time." I smiled. "Don't worry. He's okay. He'll be alright, and so will you. I know it." Without another word, Mac reached for her purse, took out her wallet, and wrote a check.

"You did it, Fiona." Her voice was low, almost a whisper, as she stared at the place her brother's solid form had been before it was gone. She turned to me, her eyes wide, and asked, "How is it I could see him? Did I imagine it?" I took the check from her and folded it slowly, trying to think of a simple answer. There wasn't one.

"I don't know. But I get the distinct impression, you saw him because he wanted you to, if only for a second."

"Will I see any more ghosts?" Mac asked. I shook my head.

"No, I don't think so. I think Jack was different because you're his blood. The same blood runs through your veins that ran through his. If that's not a link across space and time, I don't know what is." I shrugged. "But that's not important, really. What is important is the message he asked me to pass on. But before I do that, you have some news. You were bursting at the seams to tell me until you saw Jack."

"Right, yes. I did." I could see her struggling. Jack had been her brother, and her best friend. A fight had nearly torn them apart, and ripped him from her. Tears glistened in the corners of her eyes. "Did he tell you we fought? Before."

"Before he died? Yes, he told me." I took one of her hands in both of mine. "It's forgiven and forgotten, whatever it was about. He's forgiven you. It's time to forgive yourself, Maisy Catherine." I would never have used her full name if Jack hadn't suggested it.

He'd nicknamed her Mac because she was such a tomboy, but Maisy Catherine was his baby sister. A tear escaped in a single rivulet down her cheek. "Jack," she whispered. "I love and miss you, you big galoot." She'd been looking at her toes, and looked up at me again. "Thank you."

"Of course. There's more to come. I think Jack had a hunch about your news, though. So, let's have it." I sat down on the chaise, and Mac sat down next to me.

Her eyes twinkling, she explained. "As you know, I've been struggling to keep this ranch afloat. It's why I've been traveling down every revenue stream I can think of, and went into the city to meet with a couple of investors." I inhaled sharply, and she smiled. "No, these aren't sharks. These are small business owners who have become something of a collective in the community. And we've come up with a plan. Now that Jack is gone, I can ante up my part. With customers willing to return and stay in the bungalows, as well as my new event and venue set up, we my dear, are back in business!" She offered a Cheshire cat smile, and added, "Of course, there are a couple of pieces to work out..." her tone suggested I was the fish for which she'd baited the hook, and I swallowed it.

"What do you have to work out?" I asked, naively.

"I need a partner in the community who has a very special relationship to our town." She glanced at me sideways to gauge my reaction, and when none came, she added, "Plus, we're still working on the biochemical component of our new feed product... aka revenue stream. And with your... powers of... healing, you are the unicorn we're looking for, Fiona."

"Okay, I can be thick sometimes. Spit it out. I'm pretty new to town, and other than you and the realtor's name for the space in town with whom I have yet to set an appointment, I don't know a soul."

"Yes, you do. You know lots of souls." Huh? I looked at her quizzically. Where was this going?

"Mac." I gave her a look that I thought shouted *get to the point*.

"Fiona. Pay attention." Her look reflected mine. "Souls."

"Souls," I repeated. As I said it, understanding dawned. "Oh!" I gasped, my hand flying to my mouth to cover it.

"Right, you've got it! Our collective is a little more than business owners. We have a higher purpose, and we elected you, Fiona Perry, to our membership. Because there is one thing about Coloma you may have sensed, but had never put into words or solidified thoughts. This town you found yourself drawn to? I'm pretty sure there was a reason." My eyes widened and Mac laughed. "Above and beyond Jack. Though I know he's a pretty damned good reason! The truth is, this is the most haunted small town in America, and we have an ace in the hole when it comes to spirits. Souls." She paused, dramatically. I pointed to myself and raised my eyebrows to my hairline. *Me?* Mac nodded. "You."

"I. I don't know what to say. Why me? My experiment failed. Had failed. Before. I don't understand." I stood, flabbergasted, feeling an odd mix of excitement and dread. A shiver rolled down my spine, and I shook my head intending to turn tail and run.

My mouth had other plans, but thankfully, Mac stalled them. "A lot of our meetings were hashing out whether we really needed a ghost healer. After some... let's just say, unusual occurrences with our more skeptical membership, the vote was unanimous." She laughed her deep, throaty laugh, and I wondered what else had happened at the latest meeting. For the first time in a long time, Mac looked relaxed. As if she had the world at her feet. I felt flattered, sure. But I wished I felt more relieved than I did.

"I love it here, Mac. You've known that since the day we met. I knew there was a reason," I paused and laughed. "Yes, a reason beyond Jack. And now I know what I've been feeling on my walks to the river—what happened at the river's edge of your ranch?" I asked mid-sentence, a memory resurfacing from my first week or two in the bungalow.

"I don't know," she said, almost before I'd finished the sentence. "Must have been before my time." Mac rarely got cagey, but I hadn't felt threatened, just curious. I let it go. Now that I was, as Jack had so eloquently pointed out, the essence of my creation, I got the sense we were being watched. But it didn't arouse me, which was usually the case, so I ignored it, and turned back to Mac. I said, "I'm really thrilled to be included in your community this way. I hope I can live up to your expectations. This," I waved a hand around the room and at myself, "isn't an exact science."

"We are fully aware of the limitations. But we have such faith in you," Mac stood up to leave. "Take a look at that check you folded. See how strong in support we are to have you here, and as our resident ghost healer." She tilted her head, "Or do you prefer haunted house healer?"

I shrugged. "I'm not sure what to call myself, or business. The name Spectressence for my formula doesn't make sense to some, as both you and Jack both referred to it as the name of a perfume. I guess it is that now, after all!" I laughed, and for the first time in a long time, felt lighter than air. As a most unlikely biochemist with a strong spiritual side, I'd found success in the most unlikely of places. Who knew?

I felt the folded check in the palm of my hand. I'd never put it away, and at Mac's second urging, I opened it. "Mac, no! This is too much!" Dizzy at the number of zeroes, I felt faint.

"It seems the collective had been wanting to ensure JMC Ranch retained its rightful place in Coloma." She paused. "There's a secret there, but I don't think I'm privy to it. Anyway, the check was for me to do as I pleased. I knew exactly what I wanted to do with it. But I couldn't figure out how to share it with you." She held up a hand. "Forget me as client. Think of me as your friend."

"I already do." I reached out and squeezed her arm.

"I told them what you could do and explained what you had told me about why you'd come here. The fire. The lab. Ian. Your savings. Everything. I laid it all on the table for them." She looked down sheepishly and scuffed a toe into the carpet. "I was out of line, I know. But I had to make them see. And I needed their support for what I could do, too. The running of a working ranch, plus a B&B set up in ranch cottages and the main house, with places like the barn and stables to double as venues for events…"

"It's okay, Mac. It would have all come out at some point, anyway. Stuff like that doesn't stay hidden for long. Though we may want to revisit that for future reference. I don't know what the negative ramifications of Spectressence might entail or reveal. Jack was different. He was here for you. And—" I'd been rattling on, completely forgetting I hadn't told her what he wanted me to share. "That reminds me! He wanted me to give you a message. But I think it would be best to give it to you in the morning after we've both had a good night's sleep."

"Of course, you must be exhausted! But first, how about a little celebration? Will you join me in the kitchen for a glass of wine? You hosted last time. Today is my turn. Plus, I still feel bad about how things went after the bungalow incident."

"That would be wonderful! I found out the reason behind the bungalow's destruction and will tell you over wine. Can I whip something up? How about a simple charcuterie board?" I asked, wanting to be busy. My head reeling from my love-making with Jack, Mac's surprise return, and the even bigger surprise that things were looking up for Mac and JMC Ranch.

She'd paid me my fee with her portion of the check from the collective. With it, I could stick around Coloma a little longer. Now, I just had to figure out how I'd afford office space and how one goes about gaining clients. Okay, the second part wouldn't be hard. Mac knew everyone in this town; her referral would be like having a billboard. It had been one heck of a day!

"Sure," Mac called from the kitchen. She pointed to the fridge and the pantry. "Whatever you can come up with, go for it." Taking two stemless glasses from the shelf, she uncorked the bottle of Chardonnay from a nearby vineyard and poured two glasses while I chopped, sliced, and plated.

My phone buzzed just as we sat down. Ian. Now that Jack was gone, Ian didn't really have competition. But did I want or need someone to complete me? No, I was enough. I let the buzzing go to voicemail, and smiling, Mac and I toasted to new beginnings. Once the phone was quiet, and we'd had our first sips, Mac put her glass down. She ran her index finger along its rim, and asked, "I'm ready now, Fiona. What did Jack want me to know?"

I could feel his hot breath against my ear, his lips tickling as he whispered. Mac had been staring at her glass waiting for my response, so when she looked up and caught my eye, I was ready. "Jack wanted you to know a few things. But the most important is that he loves you and will watch over you, but he won't interfere. You're a strong woman who can stand on her own two feet, the result of the strong-willed little girl who didn't take no for an answer. He said also that though he won't interfere, he'll always be nearby if you need someone to talk to, he'll be listening." I paused, wondering how to present the last part. Well, there was only one way to do it: straight up, no chaser. "I'm not sure what this means, but he said I was to remember it exactly: Go to the stables, and in your horse's stall on the left side of it, under the straw in the back corner is a loose board. Pry it up. He's left you a parting gift, and that he was a jerk and you were right."

Tears streamed down Mac's face as she furiously brushed at them. "I don't even have to go. I know what's there."

"Don't you want it? Whatever it is? Jack left it for you."

"No, he didn't. My dad did. It's what we were fighting over when..." Mac put her head in her hands. "It's a stupid ring. My father's ring, yes. But nothing to fight over."

"Maybe there's something about it he wants you to see?" I suggested.

"I don't know. Maybe I'll look one of these days. But now," she raised her glass again. "Now, we have a bright future to plan for!"

My phone buzzed again, and Mac laughed. "You're not including Ian in your bright future. Are you?" I said nothing, but I hit the red decline button for the second time that day.

Chapter Fourteen

The next morning, I woke to seven missed calls. All were from Ian. I would have to deal with him sooner rather than later, but first, coffee. Mac and I had stayed up all night plotting and planning and plowing through one too many bottles of Chardonnay.

After setting the kettle to boil, I rinsed out the French press, dried it, and measured out enough grounds for two cups of coffee. Yes, both were for me. By the time I had finished breakfast, I'd have drunk two glasses of ice water, taken two pain-killers, and downed two cups of coffee. I would soon be on my way to feeling much more like myself. And abstaining from wine for a week. Well, best laid plans... c'est la vie! Whatever will be will be.

I pressed the coffee grounds into the water and watched coffee as liquid rise. The too fast pressure with the too hot water made the coffee burble over onto a coffee-stained mess on the countertop. I reached for a rag and caught sight of a headline in the paper someone had laid on my doorstep. I'd brought it in intending to read it over coffee.

"Fiona Perry, Named Riversong's Haute Kitchen's New

Executive Chef," I read out loud, my face pinched in frustration. Fingers crumpling the sheets in a slow death grip. He'd done it. Wow! I knew he had some *cojones,* but this—this, took the cake.

I crumpled the paper intent on tossing it and instead picked up the phone to press the number on one of the missed calls. Ian had forged ahead and accepted a position on my behalf. What an ass! This ends now.

"Ian," he answered.

"Dr. Ian Quigley, what are you thinking!" I raged into the phone. "I do not remember agreeing to an interview with your friend, much less an appointment as Executive Chef." I willed myself to calm down and speak rationally, though what I wanted to do was reach through the phone and wring his neck.

"But don't you see, love? It will be perfect. You can do your biochemical experiments with food. Much safer. I think they call it..." he searched for the word. "Molecular gastronomy."

"I know what they call it, Ian. I like to cook, yes. But it's a hobby. Nothing more. Besides, I have a job or rather a business. Spectressence works, whether you believe it or not. Mac has seen it in action, and has invited me into the community. So maybe I'll suggest they avoid outsiders who don't know much more than their small... circle of work, home, and peers or colleagues. I will not be moved like a piece on a chessboard to float your ego." I took a breath, and Ian stepped in.

"Are you done?" He asked, patronizing as ever.

"Yes, and so are we. Find someone else to manipulate. I'm out." I clicked the red button pining for the delicious vindication of a slammed handset into its cradle.

Once I'd calmed down, the next call I made was to Andrew Miller, the realtor whose name Mac had given me when I first moved in. "Hello, Mr. Miller. My name is Fiona

Perry. Maisy Catherine Wright gave me your phone number saying you were the man to call about an office space."

"Ah, yes! I've been expecting your call. Maisy Mac said you'd be reaching out soon. You're in luck, the space is still available, if you're interested." Maisy Mac? Usually, it was one or the other. But the Wright's had been in this town for generations. It occurred to me that most of the town had probably known her and Jack since they were born. Inside my head, I almost didn't register what he'd said. Available? Yes!

"Fantastic! Do you think I could come to see it today?" I checked my watch. "In an hour?"

"That's fine! I'll meet you at the old post office. I know you have a particular space in mind, but another has opened up which you may want to see. For comparison's sake, you understand." Two spaces were available? It had only been the one space for months. I wondered who had been in the now unoccupied space, and decided I'd ask the realtor later.

"Perfect. I'll see you, then Mr. Miller."

"Call me Andrew," he said as we hung up.

I went into the bedroom to change and caught my reflection in the mirror. My hair had kept its deepened bluish-purple tinge within the fire engine red. I'd figure out what to do with it last and stepped into the closet. Long dresses and jeans. Nope. I knew just the thing, and reaching toward the far side of the closet, I brushed past several dresses that would have been fine. But the one I wanted was a dark blue, almost black, ankle length, empire style dress. Slipping on a pair of dark shoes, I turned back toward the mirror and appraised my selection. My hair was loose, and its newfound coloring, thanks to Spectressence, could be disconcerting for some. So, I pulled it back into a simple ponytail, wrapping a black band around it like a near invisible thread keeping my hairstyle in place.

The air was brisk as I stepped outside, and I was glad I'd

remembered to grab a jacket on my way out the door. Winter's icy fingers were around the corner, and I shivered, but the autumn days were not yet lost. There were still leaves on the trees turned to harvest shades of reds and golds and greens, though most lay on the ground creating a path straight from my doorstep to the town center, and post office in which I was to meet Mr. Miller. Andrew, I reminded myself.

When I saw him, I understood why he called Mac, Maisy Mac. Andrew Miller was an older gentleman in his seventies. He had long white hair tied back, his eyebrows took up most of the top of his face, and a Colonel Sanders mustache and goatee. Dressed in a dark brown suit, out of season by a generation, he offered me his arm as I stepped forward. "You must be Miss Perry," he said with a pleasant smile. "It's a pleasure to meet you."

"Likewise," I said, taking his arm. That's when I noticed the cane hooked to his other wrist. "That's a lovely walking stick," I began, not sure if it was necessary for him to use it, or if it was a fashion accessory.

"Thank you. My wife gave it to me two Christmases ago. I never go anywhere without it."

"That's very sweet. Do you remember the space I was initially interested in?" I asked.

"Oh yes, of course. It's just a few doors down." We walked under the undercroft and into a courtyard area. Then, after passing businesses in operation, we turned off the main road, and arrived at an empty space. He took out his key and opened the door. "I have to confess. I know this isn't the one you mentioned at first. It's the other one I wanted to show you to see if you might be interested."

We stepped inside and looked around. It was a simple space. Smaller than the one into whose window I'd first peeked. But it was clean with a large desk, two chairs, and a small loveseat. "Does it come furnished?" I asked, surprised he'd show me someone's office who still had their furniture in it.

"Yes, it does," he called from a back room. "You may wish to come back here, Miss Perry. It's one of the features I wanted to show you." I followed his voice toward what I thought must be a supply closet. It surprised me to discover when I stepped in, that it was a larger room set up like a chemist's lab. I looked at Andrew sharply.

"How did you--?" I was at home here. A front office for clients and private sessions, and a back-office lab for biochemical experiments. A sense of déjà vu overcame me, and I could almost hear voices in the front, or maybe just outside the door.

"Let's just say, a little bird told me." Andrew Miller smiled coyly and ducked his head. It could only have been Mac. I didn't really know anyone else in town. I'd ask her when we finished our tour of the two offices.

Without another word, he gestured for me to follow. We left the hidden office and turned back toward the main street. A few doors down from the café was the available space I'd asked about. Once more, he took out his key, and we stepped inside the other office. "For comparison's sake," he whispered. His lips touched my ears as he spoke, his breath hot, and an old familiar feeling began to emanate from my toes up my legs. All I could think was, *no! It's not possible*.

I don't know why I hadn't sensed it earlier. My mind shouted at me; he could be your father! For shame! *Well, I can't help it*, I retorted, and prayed he didn't say anything about peppermint.

"Andrew," I began, unsure of what to say. "I think I'd like to see the other office again. It seems your instincts may have been correct regarding which office best suited my business." As we walked, he offered me his arm again, and I asked, "Do you know what my business is?"

He nodded. "Maisy Mac told me", he explained.

I frowned. "What did she say exactly?"

"She said you're a healer."

"Well, that's true. Do you know what kind of healer?" We'd come around to the first office and walked inside. This time, I took a closer look. The furniture was older, but comfortable. I tested the chairs and sat at the desk for a few minutes, imagining clients sitting across from me. Andrew had gone straight toward the lab as if he couldn't stay away. I was about to call Mac when a woman opened the door and stepped in. "Oh!" she clapped a hand to her mouth, then put it down slowly. "I'm sorry, I wasn't expecting anyone in here. Boy, they move fast in this town, don't they?" she muttered.

I jumped up. "I'm so sorry, Ms..."

"Miller. Bea Miller." She offered a dark gloved hand, and I took it.

"It's a pleasure to meet you. Are you Mr. Andrew Miller's wife? He's showing me this office to rent," I said by way of explanation. Her eyes shot up in surprise.

"That's not possible," she said. My phone rang. It was Mac.

"Mac?" I asked when I hit the green button to accept the call. "What's up? Mr. Miller is showing me a couple of offices and I've just met his wife. Can I call you back in a bit?"

"Fiona, that's why I called. Mr. Miller died this morning... I was calling to let you know I'd help you find another realtor." She paused. "Wait, did you say he'd been showing you offices? Now?" Mac's voice rose in incredulity. Then, "Does his wife know what you can do?"

"We've only just met, Mac. And until this second, I had no idea she might need my services." I looked at Mrs. Miller who had collapsed into the loveseat. "I've got to go. I'll call you later."

"Mrs. Miller! Bea! Are you okay?" I rushed to where she lay and wished I had cold water or smelling salts, or something to bring her around. Thankfully, she hadn't fainted, but was just a little woozy.

"Miss Perry!" I could hear Andrew Miller calling me from the lab. I turned toward his voice then back to Mrs. Miller.

"I'll be right back," I said. "Let me get you a glass of water." She nodded, and I headed to the backroom. When I entered, Andrew used his cane to point toward a cabinet. "I keep her pills in there." He pointed to a shelf. "There are smelling salts over there. Be careful, she gets dizzy easily." Lastly, he pointed to the corner of a metal desk pushed back against the far wall. A key lay in the middle of it. "The key is for you. I can't help you with a business name, but I can help you settle into an appropriate office. You'll be good for this town." He leaned toward me and kissed me on the forehead. "I was a chemist and a doctor before I became a realtor. You'll learn to control your impulses. But one last message for my dear Beatrice. Will you tell her for me?"

"Of course, I will. Thank you."

"Thank you, Ms. Perry. I'm ready to go, now that I know she'll be well cared for. I didn't have time to tell her before…" I nodded. When he'd gone, I took the glass of water back into the front room and gave it to Mrs. Miller.

"Thank you," she said after a few sips. "It is so strange. When I first walked in, I could have sworn he was in here with us. But now I don't feel it anymore."

I smiled. "And you won't. But he'll always be with you." I glanced back at the old chemist's lab-become-office space and then back to his wife. "I have a unique gift. Like your husband, I, too, am a chemist. I'm a biochemist, and have created a special formula, with which I can see and talk to ghosts."

Beatrice Miller didn't move, but she wasn't afraid. "Did you know this is the most haunted small town in America?" she asked in a whisper as if the ghosts might hear her.

"Yes, Mac Wright told me."

"Oh, then you must know... have known Jack," she said.

"In a way, yes."

"Did my husband say anything, Ms. Perry?" her hand gripped my wrist and squeezed, hopeful for an answer.

"Yes, he did. He showed me where your pills were, the smelling salts, and he asked me to tell you two things. He loves you and...." I stood up and went to the desk drawer, took out an envelope, and handed it to her. "To give you this."

Beatrice Miller opened the envelope with trembling hands. Inside was a key, a pressed flower, and a note. "Do you know what it means?" I asked. Her smile wide, she said, "I do indeed, Ms. Perry. He always said he'd take care of me, and with these three items, I'll be set for the rest of my life. I wish I could see him like you do, but if he's gone on to the next world, then that's even better. I'll join him soon enough." She reached in to take a few bills out of the envelope. "What do I owe?" she asked, and I waved her money away.

"Not a thing, Mrs. Miller. But if you're in agreement with Mr. Miller, I'd like to retain ownership of this," I paused. "His?" She nodded. "Office space."

"Of course, dear! What would I do with it? And please, call me Bea."

"Thank you, Bea. Please call me Fiona."

In the end it was Mrs. Miller who came up with my business name, reminiscent of a ranching brand.

3HG: Haunted Home & Ghost Healer.

Review This Book

I'm thrilled you are enjoying this book!
Reviews are my bread and butter, as an author.

Please consider using 60 seconds right now to leave a review on Amazon!

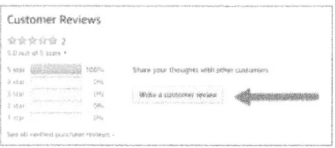

> > > **Click here to write a quick review** < < <

I'm grateful for your thoughtful review!

Even a few brief words are a useful gift for many readers!

Look For More Books
By Isabeau Durant

Please follow the links below to stay in touch and receive more!

Ghost Healer Series on Amazon

Get notified of upcoming titles by the author and publisher!

Isabeau Durant Newsletter

Printed in Great Britain
by Amazon